Destiny Road

by

Shelia Nicholson

Bloomington, IN   Milton Keynes, UK
authorHOUSE®

AuthorHouse™
1663 Liberty Drive, Suite 200
Bloomington, IN 47403
www.authorhouse.com
Phone: 1-800-839-8640

AuthorHouse™ UK Ltd.
500 Avebury Boulevard
Central Milton Keynes, MK9 2BE
www.authorhouse.co.uk
Phone: 08001974150

© 2006 Shelia Nicholson. All rights reserved.

No part of this book may be reproduced, stored in a retrieval system, or transmitted by any means without the written permission of the author.

First published by AuthorHouse 8/16/2006

ISBN: 1-4259-4706-9 (sc)

Library of Congress Control Number: 2006906461

Printed in the United States of America
Bloomington, Indiana

This book is printed on acid-free paper.

This book is dedicated to my loving husband,

Wendell Nicholson

Who has always been my best friend.

Without his companionship and guidance while researching points of interest, this book would never have been written.

Psalm 86:12 "I will praise you, O Lord my God, with all my heart; I will glorify your name forever."

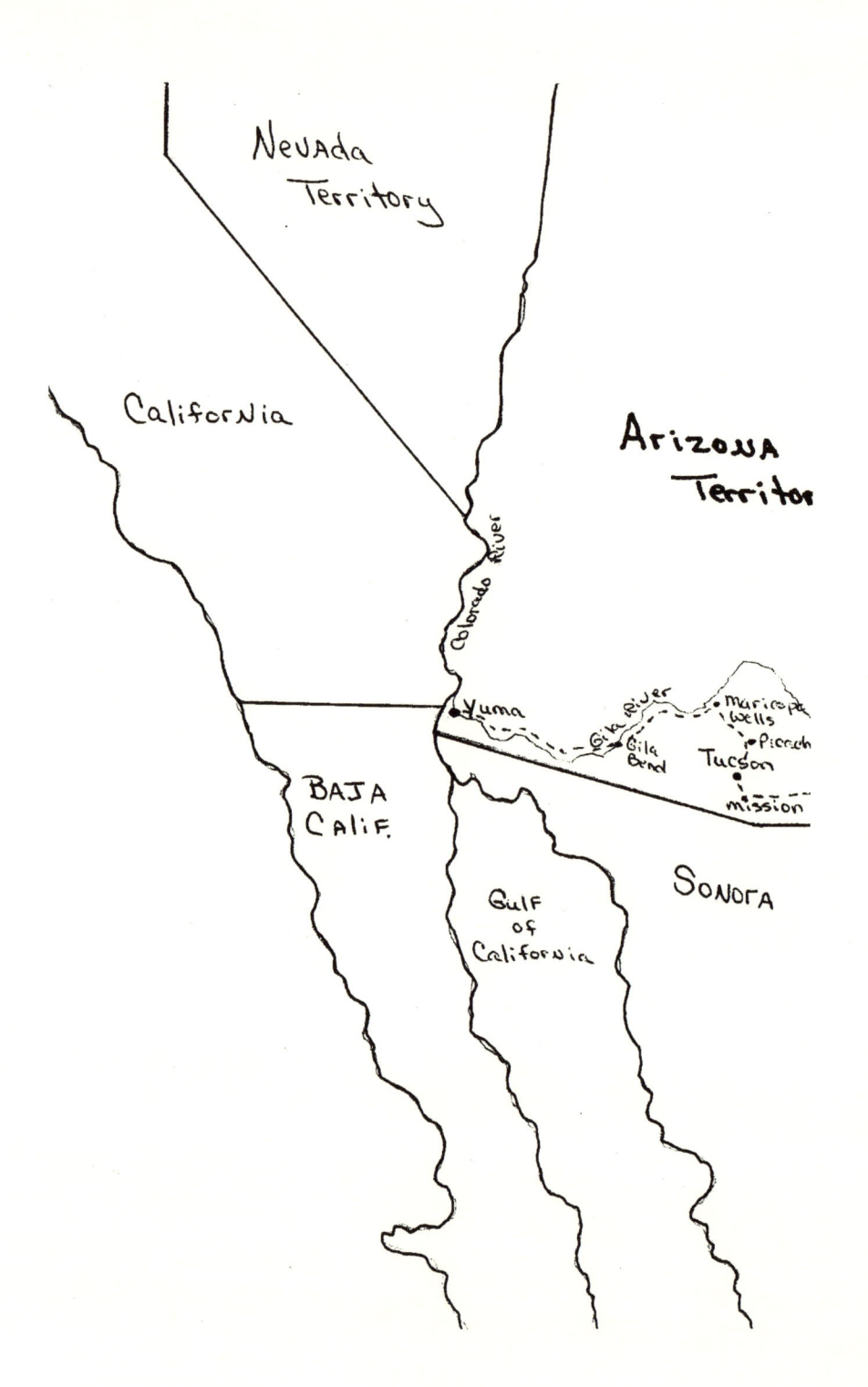

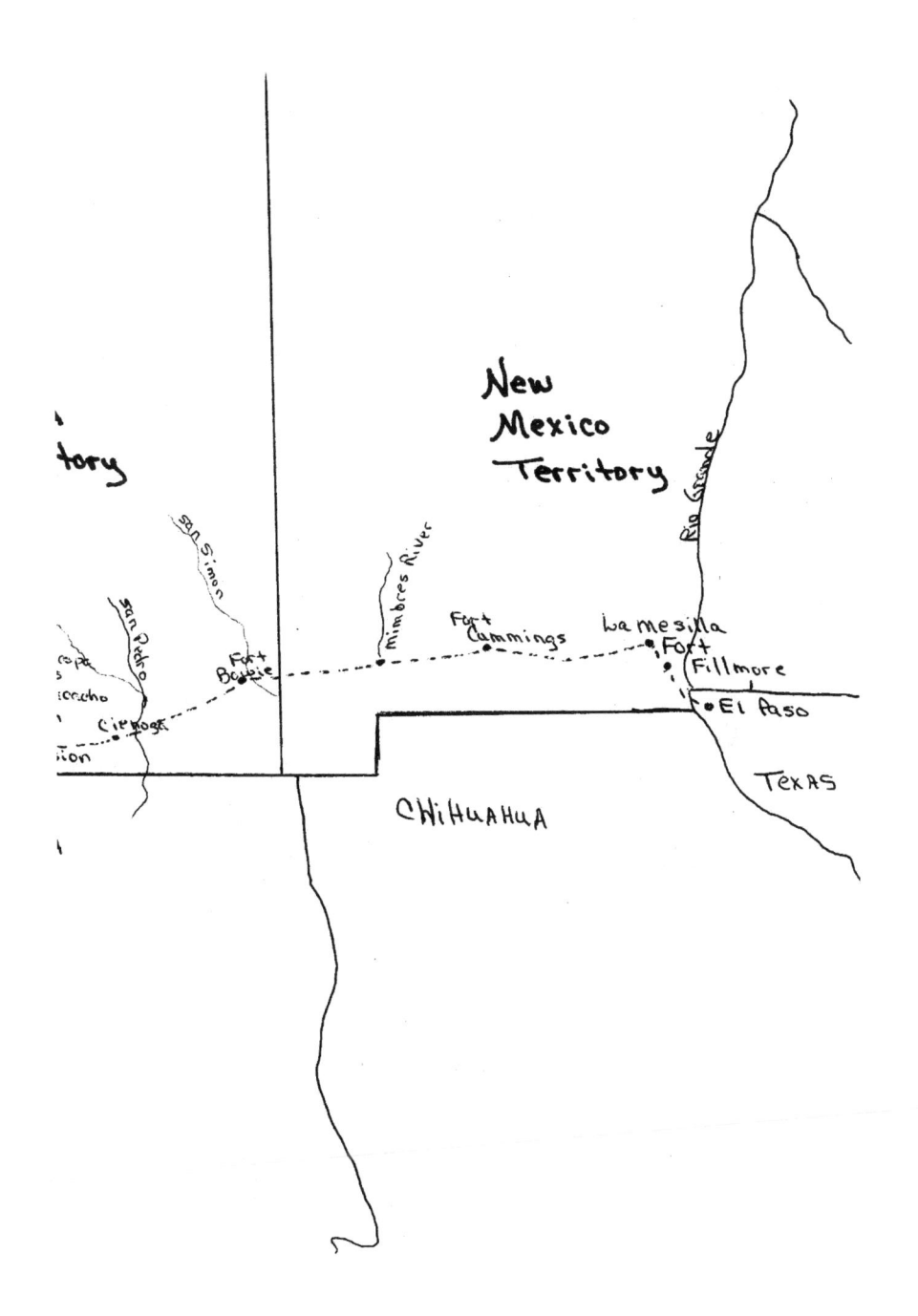

IN APPRECIATION

To our Loving God,
Who gave us such a wonderful land of many opportunities, and, to all of the thousands of Pioneers, some willing, some against their will, who bravely paved and tamed the way West for all of us to enjoy and live in peace today.

Also, a special thanks to the many friends and loved ones who have helped me edit and research the history of certain areas.

To name a few:
Mary Gray, my kindred spirit;

Roy Worley, my wonderful son-in-law, who taught me more about computers than I ever wanted to know!

> My editors and "proof" readers:
> Gwen Davis
> Jack Davis
> Clifton Tuggle
> Roy Webster
> Robert Zimmerman

Others who supplied me with maps and interesting facts of particular areas:
> Jean Fulton, who helped with information on the South Texas Missions,
> Ken Kesselsus, from Bastrop, Texas,
> Barbara Vanna, Bastrop, Texas, and
> Stan Wallace, my brother from Schertz, Texas.

There are undoubtedly others who have unselfishly tried to answer my millions of questions whose names I probably never knew.

My apologies for not naming you,
But many, many thanks for your help, also.

CHAPTER ONE

As I slid my pack over my shoulder, I realized just how tired I was. The last four years now felt like forty. The War Between the States was finally over, and General Edmund Kirby Smith had finally surrendered the last Confederate Army in May, 1865.

I was there when General Robert E. Lee walked his horse down the lane at Appomattox Courthouse, and surrendered to General Ulysses S. Grant. That had been on a Sunday, April 9, 1865.

We had been Hood's Texas Brigade. When we started out, we thought the war would last only a couple of months, six at the most. We were returning home with only 143 men and 15 officers out of 1,343 soldiers.

I had seen a lot of Texas boys die on battlefields and had been in so many battles myself that I couldn't even remember them all.

Now home was just over the next river. I was taking a ferry over the Red River in Louisiana, and then I would almost be home on the Little Cypress Bayou in Texas. Most of the Southern soldiers began singing "The Yellow Rose of Texas." I joined in weakly, though I really didn't feel much like singing at all.

I had been raised on a farm just north of the town of Marshall by my aunt and uncle after my parents had been killed by the Kickapoo Indians when I was a baby. They had left me with my aunt and uncle when they moved to Nacogdoches to go to work for a new mercantile store. But their wagon was found burned, and their bodies mutilated. The two other families with them met with a similar fate.

My childhood memories were only of my aunt and uncle, and their daughter, Anne. We worked hard, played hard, and for the most part had a fairly normal life.

I had not heard from Uncle William and Aunt Kate since I left for the war in 1861. My uncle and I had always gotten along fine, but I always felt a little bit in the way with Aunt Kate. Life was hard in Texas before the war, and it made hard people. I can't recall my aunt smiling very much, or even acting like she was ever really happy. There was always so much work to be done, that if anyone ever took an afternoon off to go fishing or just relax, that person was looked upon as being just plain lazy! And my aunt had a way about her that gave the impression that she thought a lot of people were lazy.

It was late afternoon when I topped the ridge and looked down on the picturesque scene. I had no idea what to expect. Unbelievably, everything looked almost the same.

Uncle William came out of the barn just as I was coming through the gate. He stopped dead still and just stared at me for a moment.

"Uncle William!" I hollered out as I ran up to him.

"Tad boy?" he stuttered. "Is that you? Is the war over?" We stood and hugged for a moment.

"You left here just a boy, and now just look at ya! You're all growed up!"

"Where's Aunt Kate?" I asked while looking around.

His eyes could not meet mine, and I immediately knew something was wrong. "She died some time back of the fever," he answered weakly. Pointing limply, he added, "She's buried over there in the family plot, next to yore parents."

As I looked in the direction to which his gnarled finger pointed, I saw some roses planted there that I didn't remember being there before. A small hand- carved marker now stood beside my mother's. My father's marker was on the other side. A neat wire fence with a gate on one side had been erected around the area. I also noted that there was room left for about four more graves.

"Anne and her family are moving out here to live with me and help me on the old place. Her husband, Robert, came home last week. We didn't know what had happened to you, but now that you're here, we'll just have more help."

It was good to be home. I felt like I could have lain down and slept for a month.

Anne was their only daughter. She was a couple of years older than me, but we had been as close as any brother and sister could have been. She had married about a year before the war broke out, and now she had two children. I had never seen either of them. Robert Lang, her husband, had never liked me much. She had done her best to make us friends, but all of her efforts had been of no avail. He had never liked to be outdoors hunting or fishing, but had preferred to stay in the house and read. I couldn't believe it when I heard that he had joined the Cause and had been deployed to the Galveston area. I was anxious to see if the war had changed him.

I didn't have to wait too long, for they came in their wagon the very next day. I was in the barn mending some of Uncle William's bridles when I heard the wagon pull up. The squeal of children filled the air, and Uncle William seemed to be the happiest man alive.

Robert was helping Anne out of the wagon when we saw each other.

"Tad! I can't believe it's you," cried Anne as she came running up to hug me.

She looked older, and I could tell that the war had been hard on her.

"Hello Robert! It's good to see you again," I said amiably, trying not to stare at the obviously limp sleeve. He had lost his left arm.

"Tad, you look as tired as I feel," he said slowly. "I'm just ready to get back to plowing and building things, instead of blowing up the world. Do you think things will ever be the same?"

I wanted to tell him, "No, the South could never be the same," but the words just wouldn't come. All I could get out was, "We'll try."

During the next few days we got Robert and Anne settled into the house, and she began to make the kitchen her own. Within a couple of weeks it seemed as if they had been there for years. Anne and I had planted a small garden, and the children were delighted with new baby chicks. It was June, 1865, and I began to feel out of place.

Nothing was said at first, but I began to feel more and more restless. One evening, after supper, Uncle William began telling one of his stories about his brother Emmit who had gone out West on a survey party back in the 1840s. He had written home telling about deserts, mountains, Indians, and all types of fascinating people. He made the West sound wonderful. I finally broke the news that I thought I might go west and see the world before settling down.

Uncle William told me that he'd noticed I had seemed restless since arriving home, and maybe this was a good time to get away on my own for awhile.

They cried and pleaded for me to stay, but in the end helped me pack my few belongings. Anne gave me a new pair of socks she had knitted and made me a new shirt. Uncle William let me have one of his mustang ponies and a poke of food for a grubstake.

On a bright summer morning I began to make my way to the town of Marshall. I knew of a road to Nacogdoches, and then the Old San Antonio Road would take me all the way to San Antonio. It was sounding like a grand trip, and I was looking forward to seeing the West.

CHAPTER TWO

Jasper placed the last heavy river rock on the small grave. This was the third grave he had dug in as many weeks. Men could fight other men in wars, they could even fight the renegades that had swept through the land like locusts, but they couldn't fight the Typhoid Fever.

The year was 1865, and the War Between the States had ended one month earlier. The plantation that Jasper had lived on had seen dramatic changes in the past four years. The cotton fields had not been worked for a couple of years now, and it seemed like everything could use a coat of paint. The animals were almost all gone, either taken by the armies or eaten for food.

The plantation's "Big House" consisted of nine rooms. Four bedrooms were located on the second floor, while the reception hall, dining room, parlor, library, and the serving kitchen were all located on the first floor. The cookhouse was a separate building between the house and the slave quarters. Attached was the sewing and weaving room. The dyeing of the yarn was done beneath a long porch.

The outside of the house was the traditional Greek revival look that most of the mansion owners of the deep-south had favored. The huge columns and once beautiful porch were in sad need of repair. The sprawling lawns that had once been immaculately maintained were non-existent now. There was no difference between the road that led up to the house and the lawn. All was gravel and dirt!

Jasper Barker, (he had taken the last name of his owner as most slaves did), was an exceptionally big man, well over six feet tall, with muscles bulging beneath his shirt. He had been the overseer of the animals since his early teens. Other slaves worked in the fields or in the house, but his duties had always been with the animals. He had a way with them, especially horses and mules. The only animals left now were two mules and a cow with a new calf.

The forty slaves that had belonged to the Barker family all lived in the cabins about 200 yards from the main house. The Emancipation Proclamation issued by President Lincoln had freed them, or so they thought. It declared that all slaves were to be free, and "were to labor faithfully for reasonable wages". Jasper and Selena, his wife, had remained alone on the big place to help the aging couple with their twin granddaughters.

Selena was born on a nearby plantation, but had been bought by the Barkers, along with her parents, almost 15 years ago when still a child. Being tall, but very thin all of her life, she was used as a house servant. She was at first expected to help dress the twin granddaughters, Lena and Emma. As the years went by she took on more responsibility, but became fast friends with the twins and felt that she was actually treated as one of the family.

Then the war had come, and the fever had followed. Jasper and Selena found themselves in a situation that they could never have foreseen. In the past few weeks the entire family, except for Miss Emma and her father (who was out west in California), had succumbed to the Typhoid Fever. How in the world had it all come to this?

Their home in East Texas was called the Pecan Grove Plantation. They had never been more than 20 miles away from it in any direction their entire lives. Jasper sat down to reflect on the situation in which they now found themselves.

Toward the end of the war Master Barker told Jasper and Selena that they were free to go, and that even if he wanted to keep them under his employment, there was no money. Jasper had often dreamed of being free, owning his own land, raising his own crops. But he also remembered his home here. One side of him wanted to run and be away from anything that reminded him of slavery. The other side saw two old people that had always been fair to him and the other slaves.

He knew from visiting slaves from other plantations, that good treatment did not always happen. He particularly remembered driving the family to a big dinner one evening. While taking care of the team, the others told stories about beatings and horrible atrocities that made the hair stand up on Jasper's neck!

When he and Selena "jumped the broom" (got married), Selena took over the duties of looking after the two granddaughters, even though she was only a few years older than they. They had grown to love and share things of everyday life with Selena.

The girls were the 16-year-old twin granddaughters of the Barkers. Their mother had died in childbirth. Their father, Richard Barker, had gone to California in 1860 with a partner to begin a vineyard near San Diego. Then the war changed everything. His original plans were to send for his daughters as soon as he got settled out West. But, in November 1861, Richard Barker enlisted in the California Volunteers Company K. Like many men, he felt it his duty to fight for what he thought was right.

His letters, that came none too often, told of thrilling tales of fighting the Indians on the Eel River and other engagements. But his unit never left California the entire four years of the Civil War. His last letter stated he was to be mustered out of the service, and that he was somewhere near San Francisco.

Life had been easy for the Barkers, as he had been very successful in the cotton trade. He was also well respected in community politics. They loved to give big parties and dinners and entertained lavishly.

Mrs. Ethel Barker was an efficient woman, who liked to see things run smoothly. She made sure that the slaves were properly clothed and fed, and, if any fell ill, did not hesitate to call for the doctor.

She felt fortunate that one of the slaves, Martha, was an expert at dyeing cotton. She knew all about the roots, berries, and leaves that made any color they needed. Martha bragged that she could make any color in the rainbow. They had a special room, set up just for the spinning of the cotton, which adjoined the outside cookhouse.

There wasn't much difference in the running of things when the war first started, but as the years dragged on, things got continually worse. Toward the end, there were no new clothes, and not even enough food for everyone. A few of the slaves decided to run off. With no money the Barkers could not afford to keep them anyway.

It had been amazing to see a place as splendid as the Barkers' fall completely apart in just four short years. The house and outbuildings looked as if it had not seen any paint in twenty years, and the fields appeared as if they had not been worked in ten. Even the trees that had been so carefully cleared had begun to creep back. Weeds, that the field overseer would never have allowed, were almost shoulder tall.

With stories of renegade soldiers terrorizing the land, slaves rebelling against unmerciful owners, news of men they knew being killed on battlefields, made the Barkers feel things couldn't get much worse. Then the news that President Lincoln had been assassinated came. Being Southerners, the Barkers hadn't agreed with all of his policies. But for a President of the United States to be shot was unimaginable. Then the dreaded Typhoid Fever came. Across the land, whole communities were infected. Mr. Barker was the first one to succumb to the fever. But before he died, he had asked Jasper, strictly as a favor to him, to see that his family was taken to Richard out in California. His last wish was for Jasper to have a small wooden chest, which he said would help him on the journey. All Jasper knew of California was that it was a long way off.

The next Monday they buried Mrs. Barker. The fever knew no favorites. Jasper and Selena worked night and day to save Lena, Emma's twin, but survivors were few with this dreaded disease. Her small grave was the last one in the fenced-in family plot.

Jasper made headstones out of wood boards that he took from the barn door. Miss Emma helped him with the spelling of the names' since Jasper could neither read nor write. It was against the law to teach a slave to read or write in most states in 1865.

As the three of them finished saying goodbye to Lena and turned to leave the family plot, a neighbor, Robert Taggert, raced into the yard on a terrified horse! "Renegades! Just burned my place! On their way here!" he gasped out in short breaths. As they were helping the wounded man down, he collapsed in Jasper's arms.

Jasper quickly took everyone, including the animals, up to a cave nearby that he had found several years earlier. He had had a feeling that the end of the war might bring more trouble to the plantation, so he had made some preparations some time back. The wounded neighbor was now laid down on some straw that Jasper had stashed there as food for the animals.

The renegades did come, and finding very little to take, torched the beautiful house. All Jasper, Selena, and Emma could do was watch from a distance, as their home slowly burned to embers. Deep in their own thoughts and memories, each felt helpless as they saw the fire spread throughout the old place.

The next day as they walked through the ruins and ashes, Jasper decided it was time to fulfill Master Barker's wishes and take Emma, the last of the family, to her father. Mr. Taggert, whom they had nursed back to health, presented them with a small buckboard wagon, but he had no horses or oxen to give them. The mules they had used to plow the fields would just have to do for now.

Jasper went to the cave for the last ham and pork-shoulder that they had managed to hide, carefully wrapped them in cheese-cloth, and loaded them into the small wagon.

Selena found a frying pan, two Dutch ovens, a coffee pot, and some eating utensils that were in some of the slaves' quarters behind the big house. Emma went down into the storm shelter and found several old quilts that her grandmother and mother had lovingly made. Jasper helped the women pack these few belongings into the wagon.

As if in a trance, with soot-smudged faces and tracks of tears, Jasper drove the group out of the yard and down the road. Emma sat in the back where she could watch the spot where her home had been get smaller and smaller, until it was finally out of sight. The last thing she could see was the family cemetery on top of the hill. She silently told them, each, farewell one last time.

CHAPTER THREE

The first stop was in the town of Marshall. Miss Emma and Jasper went into the general store in hopes of trading for some provisions. They were starting out on the journey with very little food. Jasper was hoping there would be game along the way for fresh meat. They were literally trusting in the Almighty to help provide for them.

Jasper's size being what it was, people just naturally moved aside for him. He opened the door to the store and escorted Miss Emma inside.

"Good morning, Mr. Price," Emma said sweetly in her southern drawl.

"Well, Miss Emma Barker. We sure were sorry to hear about your grandparents and sister. Times are very hard on folks these days," Mr. Price replied.

Emma fought back the tears that were filling her eyes again. "They are indeed. We have decided to go to my father out in California.

There is nothing here for us anymore. But we need a few supplies before we can start out on such a journey."

She had never done business with Mr. Price; her grandfather and father had always taken care of such matters. If truth be told, she never really cared for him. He talked very rudely to people if he thought he were better than they.

"Do you have gold? You do know, of course, that Confederate money isn't worth the paper it's printed on!" he said abruptly.

"Well," she started hesitantly, "we were hoping to trade."

"Trade? Trade what?" Mr. Price was sounding more exasperated by the minute.

Jasper laid the old shotgun on the counter. The proprietor almost laughed out loud, but caught himself. Emma reached into her bag she was carrying and pulled out two beautiful matching pearl-handled pistols.

His eyes softened. "These were your grandfather's, weren't they?" he asked softly.

"Yes, they were among his favorite possessions," she answered proudly. "We also have a cow and a calf that we need to either sell or trade."

"Well, I think we can indeed do some trading, young lady," Doyle Price answered as if seeing her in a whole new light. In no time at all Jasper was loading sides of bacon, hams, sacks of flour and dried beans, and some dried apples into the small wagon.

"Thank you very much, Mr. Price. This will really help us," said Emma. She was trying to be very brave about losing her grandfather's pistols, but she saw no other way. They needed the supplies.

"I wish I could do more, but the war has left Texas just about bare," he answered as he handed her two small sacks. "Your family was always good to help out when folks here needed a helping hand. This isn't much, just a little luxury for you on your way," he added. Then he reached over and handed Jasper back the old shotgun, and reached behind him for a box of shells. "This might come in handy for bird hunting along the way."

Jasper and, all the others in the room were well aware that slaves were never given guns because most of the white folks feared the thought of it. But, all here knew that Jasper had gone hunting with Mr. Barker for several years, and had been seen bird hunting many times with that shotgun. "Thank ya, suh" was all Jasper could get out.

"Well, good luck to you folks, and give your father greetings from us," said Mr. Price as he stood at the door and watched them finish loading. Deep in his own thoughts, Doyle Price slowly walked back into his store.

Unobserved, a figure moved out of a corner of the store. "That was mighty nice of you to help them out that way." Startled, Mr. Price whirled around, totally unaware that anyone else was in the store.

"Her father and I were good friends," he answered softly. Then resuming his businesslike voice, "How can I help you today?" he asked.

Tad Cummings gave him his small order. As he was waiting, he stepped to the window and watched the group outside tying things down on the wagon getting ready to leave.

"They're going to have a hard time getting to California," Price said absentmindedly.

"Why do you think that?"

"A white girl, alone, with two darkies?"

"The war is supposed to be over," was the tired answer.

"It's not over that much!"

Tad paid his bill, picked up his small sack, and walked out onto the street. His horse had been patiently waiting, tied to the rail in front of the general store.

The saddle bags were a long way from being full, even with his new purchases stashed inside. He now had coffee, canned beans, and some dried apples that would get him down the road for awhile.

He decided that one last drink in the saloon, and maybe picking up on some news would help get him started on his trip west. Walking across the street, he had to pass the small wagon that was still being readied for the journey.

His eyes locked with Emma's for one brief second.

He smiled and tipped his hat. She gave a nod of acknowledgment and promptly turned back to her work. He couldn't help but feel uneasy about the trio.

Captain Tad Cummings would never forget her blond hair, blue eyes, or even the yellow gingham bonnet she was wearing that day. His ego would have probably been crushed if he had known that Emma had not particularly noticed anything about him.

"Captain Cummings! Is that you? How about this?" A young officer hurried across the street, his hand held out.

"Doc Turner! You ol' cuss! Where did you come from?" was Captain Cumming's greeting back to him.

Old! Emma thought to herself. He was one of the most handsome men she had ever seen.

He stood just a little under six feet tall. His light brown, curly hair had become sun bleached from too many hours outdoors.

He, like so many others, was still wearing what was left of his confederate uniform.

He and the captain went on inside the Golden Slipper saloon to have a drink and remember old times. They had first met in 1863 on a battlefield in North Carolina. Tad Cummings had been wounded in the shoulder and this young doctor was the one who had treated him.

"Hey! How about something for the pain?" Captain Cummings had yelled.

Doc Turner tried to explain, "I'm very sorry sir, but we have nothing! Our supply trains keep getting captured and the railroad keeps getting blown up. It's a wonder there is even enough ammunition to keep this war going! But, unfortunately, there seems to be plenty of that!"

They ran into each other several other times over the course of the next two years. Their units always seemed to be in close proximity. They found out quite a lot about each other during their visits and laughed that they had absolutely nothing in common!

Tad Cummings had been raised dirt poor in Texas by hardworking farmers. Dr. Matt Turner had been raised on a beautiful plantation in South Carolina. Over this last drink together, though, they had finally discovered they did have something in common after all. They had both lost all they had during the War Between the States.

Dr. Turner had been raised in the South, but had been educated in the North. One of the brightest students of his class, he felt his career was over when the war began. He remained at a hospital in New York for the first two years of the war, justifying his noninvolvement by thinking that the war would only last a few months at best. Then he received word that the family plantation had been burned, and all his family had died of smallpox.

The land was now being assigned to freemen under General Sherman's famous "Order No.15." The Freedman's Bureau had taken over more than a million acres of plantation lands that had been abandoned by the planters who had fled the Union Armies along the coastal rivers of Georgia and South Carolina.

With everyone in his family gone along with the land, Matt Turner said out loud, "I really don't have anywhere to go. What about you?"

Tad Cummings gazed into the mirror over the bar for a minute. "Several years ago, I had an uncle that had been on one of those survey parties in the Southwest. When I was a kid, I could listen all day about his stories of the West. He made it all sound so adventurous and exciting. I've wanted to go out there ever since."

"Rattlesnakes and Indians!" exclaimed Doc Turner. "That's all I've heard about the West!" He added as he tossed of the last of his drink. He then leaned heavily on the bar, and stared blankly into the empty glass. "You know, at the beginning of the war, only a handful of doctors volunteered, because no one thought it would last over six months! We sure were a cocky lot! Then, towards the end, there were probably thousands of doctors and nurses on both sides, and even that wasn't near enough. Now that the war is finally over, we're to just shake it off, and start all over again. How do you do that?" The question seemed to lay heavy in the air.

"Well, I've been thinking something serious about it, Captain Cummings replied with a tilt in his voice (trying to improve his friend's mood). "I've decided that I'm young, free, and twenty-one and I think I'll head to California! Want to come?" He added while setting his glass down a little too hard on the bar.

"I happen to know that you are closer to 31! But if a man can't be free and go where he wants to, what's the use of living, Eh?" So much had happened in Doc Turner's young 26 years. He felt much older. The war had changed everyone and everything. Nothing would ever be the same for anyone who had experienced it.

It was a mutual decision to travel on together, and share whatever supplies they had been able to gather up.

The road outside of town was crowded and muddy. Horsemen and wagons full of families were making deep ruts deeper. Texas had been poor before the war. Now it seemed beyond regeneration.

Everyone was dressed in rags. Many were walking and most of them were barefoot. But in everyone's mind and heart there was hope for a new beginning.

The transcontinental telegraph was being strung up across the West to San Francisco. The great railroads were in the process of being built. The Union Pacific managed to lay just 40 miles of track before the surrender at Appomattox. The Central Pacific was coming to meet it from the west. Towns way out west were springing up as if by magic. All over the United States, lives that had been interrupted by the war were resuming again.

The two men rode on, each deep in his own thoughts. The aroma of coffee and frying bacon filled the air. Suddenly through the brush that grew beside the trail, they caught sight of a small campfire. The fire and aromas were tantalizing.

"Lordy, I'm hungry. Haven't eaten since breakfast," Tad said.

"You suppose they might share some of that coffee?" Doc asked almost in a whisper.

Carefully approaching the area Tad called out, "Hello to Camp!" Nothing moved. They inched a little closer and called out again.

It was a time when no one trusted anyone. The war had left scars on everyone that would take generations to erase, if ever.

Suddenly a huge black man appeared from the darkness with a shotgun in front of him!

"Wuz you want?" was the flat-voiced question. Doc Turner swallowed hard. The man was a Hercules. His black skin looked darker than ever in the glow of the campfire. His homespun clothes

Destiny Road

were typical of slaves, while suspenders were helping to keep the large baggy pants around his waist. Tad, taking it all in, wondered where in the world boots that large could be found.

Beyond him, they could make out a small wagon. Beside him was a young, petite, blonde woman that didn't even come up to his elbow.

"So, we meet again," the young woman was saying as she walked toward them.

Captain Cummings gathered himself first, and put out a hand to greet hers. "Howdy, ma'am. We almost met this afternoon. I'm Captain Tad Cummings. This is Dr. Matt Turner. Captain Cummings couldn't help but keep glancing at Jasper, just to keep an eye on him and that shotgun. "It's been a mighty long day and a might longer since we've tasted coffee."

"Then get down and set awhile. We've enough to spare," the pretty young woman said.

Matt Turner couldn't have cared less about Jasper. He was looking into the bluest eyes this side of the Mississippi.

Selena busied herself around the campfire, bringing the newcomers coffee, a plate of bacon and some bread. Everyone began to relax a little. Emma was busy hanging quilts around the bottom of the wagon, so she and Selena could go to bed in privacy. Jasper intended to sleep on the ground and keep a wary eye out at night.

As they ate, Miss Emma told them of their good fortune in being given a small packet of coffee and sugar. "For several months now, we've only had parched corn for coffee, and sugar has been gone for years, it seems, so this is really a treat for us!" The men shared some similar stories of rations in the army, and tensions began to ease a little more.

But Jasper trusted no one and wished that Miss Emma wouldn't tell these strange men all about their trip and business. He finally laid the shotgun down, but made sure it was always in reach.

Tad Cummings had not missed a thing. He realized that this black couple loved this girl and would protect her to the death.

Tad and Matt told the group of their plans to go west in just general conversation.

"We, too, are going west. To California, to my father," Emma said. "It was my grandfather's dying wish that Jasper and Selena help me get there. Have you been to California before?" she asked. They talked on into the night about each other's plans.

While saddling their horses the next morning, Tad and Matt decided to ask the group if they would like to ride together for awhile. It was quite obvious that they, too, had been thinking about the same thing.

Tad recommended the best road for them to travel on would be the Old San Antonio Road. He had been on this road several times before the war, and had been all the way to San Antonio a couple of times. There would be rivers to cross and unknown hardships all the way, but at least he knew this part of the country.

After San Antonio they would all be in unknown territory. They would need some help or a map, but they would face that problem when they came to it. Nacogdoches was their first destination.

Destiny Road

Tad knew all too well that the Kickapoo Indians still lived around the area, and that during the war they had in fact attacked a troop of Confederates near this road.

On the first evening out, Tad reached over to grab a water bucket off the wagon intending to water the horses and mules. Suddenly a huge hand shot out and snatched the bucket right out of his hands! Startled, Tad found himself looking up at Jasper's big frame.

"Dis bucket's Miss Emma's," explained a calm, deep voice. Reaching over to another larger bucket, he handed it to Tad, "Water de mules wi' dis one."

Emma couldn't help but hear the conversation. She realized for the first time that she was still being treated like a little princess. Jasper and Selena had taken care of her family for so long they couldn't imagine not doing so. Emma resolved that she would do her part of the work on this trip and stop expecting such special treatment.

They were averaging ten to twelve miles a day. Surprisingly, the roads had not been too bad. In fact, they seemed rather well traveled. They had already seen some cattle herds heading for the California gold fields and at least two different wagon trains consisting of at least twenty-five wagons in each group.

After Nacogdoches, they turned somewhat west, and got on the well-traveled road that they had been looking for. Other names for this road were *El Camino Real*, or the "Kings Highway". It was ages old and followed ancient Indian and buffalo trails. It stretched over a thousand miles all the way from Mexico to Louisiana.

By now they had depleted their supplies some, and were beginning to feel the emotions they had repressed since their hasty departure. The hard events had happened so quickly, they had not taken much time for grief.

In the middle of the night one evening, Emma was awakened out of a troubled sleep by a muffled sound. She dared not move, but lay perfectly still trying to determine where the sound was coming from.

After a few seconds, she realized that Selena, lying near her, was sobbing quietly into her pillow. Emma put a gentle hand on her shoulder, and without a word, the two young women wept and hugged each other in the early hours of the morning. When Selena's tears were dry and emotions under better control, Selena tenderly took Emma's hands into hers and cautioned, "You must never tell of our tears to the men."

"I know," was the solemn answer.

During the past few weeks their lives had changed more than either could have ever imagined. Emma could hardly accept the fact that everyone in her family was gone and that she would never see them, touch them, or to hear their voices again. What she had not considered until this very moment was that Selena had lost her home, too. She was feeling the same deep grief for family members that Emma felt.

Traveling began to get easier for the women as they got more used to the swaying and bouncing of the wagon. They found that they enjoyed walking beside the wagon and could easily keep up.

Emma also found that Selena and Jasper were quite used to cooking "on the ground", as it was called. Selena reminded her that most of the cooking on the plantation had been done that way as it was usually too hot in the summer to cook inside the cooking kitchen. Emma was a little embarrassed to realize that she had never really thought about how a meal was prepared. It had always been put in pretty bowls and on platters and was already on the table when she was seated.

She could envision in her mind the butler's pantry that held all of the serving dishes, all of them shining through the cabinet's glass doors. There had been a "dumb waiter" that would lift their tea sets up to the second floor. What a grand life it had been!

She could still see Grandfather seated at the head of the table as always. He looked so handsome in his red waistcoat and starched white shirt. He always appeared stern and serious, but Emma knew another side of him. She knew the side that stroked her hair when he talked to her and patted the cat that loved to lie in his lap, and the side of him that lovingly watched his beautiful wife from across the room.

Ah! Grandmother! What a lovely lady! Emma secretly envied everything about her, and hoped someday to be just like her. She had been graceful in every movement, always dressed in such beautiful dresses, never too elaborate, just enough. And, as always, there were her pearls!

Sounds of the camp suddenly brought Emma back to the present, and she realized that she had been daydreaming. She knew her past life could never exist again, and to dwell on the past would only bring unhappiness to everyone. But she was very happy to have been able to have known such wonderful grandparents, and to be able to have such memories.

She also realized that she would have to change and help the others if they were to get to California safely. It was a long way off, and she had heard that such a trip could take up to three months. She had no idea how they were going to do it, but she felt more confident having Captain Cummings and Doc Turner along with them.

The Angelina River was the first to be crossed, and they accomplished it quite easily. The water level had already gone down from the spring floods, and the river was quite narrow at the crossing. It gave them all a false confidence that all of the rivers would be easily forded this time of year.

The next river was the Neches, and Tad remembered hearing of a ferry crossing there. The barges carrying cotton bales down to the coast before the war now carried a multitude of soldiers back home. The shouts of men, the braying of mules and the clatter of wagons was nearly deafening.

Several seedy-looking characters were loitering around. The men couldn't decide if they were there to rob people or were just down on their luck since the war. A lot of people they had met on the road were dressed in rags and were barefoot.

A small community was established on the bank where few supplies were available to the travelers. Tad and Matt decided to go see if there was anything they could afford. Jasper decided he would stay with the wagon and women.

All of the supplies were outrageously expensive. Captain Cummings and Doc Turner did what they could, but they had not been paid for months toward the end of the war. There was very little money between the two of them, and they had nothing to trade. Captain Cummings had only his horse and his revolver, which, as an officer, he was able to keep after the war. He and Doc Turner each carried a Bowie knife, and Doc Turner also carried a revolver. These were their few belongings. They made their way back to the riverbank to tell the group how bad things were.

Jasper and Selena were nowhere in sight, but they found Emma in a heated discussion with two ruffians. "Actually," she was saying almost casually, "I'm with them, not the other way around. They are taking me to my father. And this is our camp, and you have not been invited here. So please leave." The hard cases were dumbfounded that a young slip of a girl would talk to them this way and began to laugh.

Matt and Tad stepped behind a large tree with their revolvers drawn. At first they were mildly amused by the entire affair.

The men ceased to laugh when Emma leveled the old shotgun that lay hidden in the folds of her skirts at the men's stomachs.

"Now wait a minute missy! We're just being friendly!" they began to protest while backing up.

"I'm not!" she said seriously, holding the shotgun more firmly.

"Why, we's jest wonderin' why a purty little thang like you was with them nig---." Their words stopped short as she took deadly aim at the center of the men.

Before someone got seriously hurt, Tad decided to let their presence be known. "Hello to camp!" he announced as he and Doc Turner walked up as if nothing were happening.

"Hello gents, can we help you today?" Tad asked as he reached over and took the shotgun from Emma. Her limp arms fell lifeless to her sides.

"No, no, we're just passing by…trying to be friendly…." They turned and almost ran over each other leaving. Doc was helping Emma to sit down when Tad finally turned to look. Big grins were on the men's faces, but they decided now was not the time to tease her.

"We left Jasper here to look out for things while we were gone. Where is he?" Matt finally asked almost angrily.

"Selena wanted him to help her take the clothes down to the water for her. But that was some time ago now," Emma replied with alarm. Captain Cummings checked his revolver and asked Doc Turner laughingly, "Would you mind watching out for Emma while I go check on the others?"

Jasper had gone earlier with Selena at her request. The river bank was muddy, slippery and slightly steep in some places. It took them a good thirty minutes just to walk down to the water. Selena was completely out of breath when they finally made it, so Jasper ended up doing most of the washing of the clothes. While helping wring out the wet clothes, she had confided in him that she was sure she was with child. Jasper was both elated and scared to death. What a time! Here they were in the middle of Indian country, with no home of their own!

"I's mighty glad we got a doc along wid us!" Jasper said out loud to himself more than to Selena.

At that suggestion, Selena made a chuckle. "He's been one of them army doctor's most of his life, he's likely never even held a baby!"

"Aw 'de same, I'se glad he's here," answered a nervous Jasper.

As was the custom of the time, Selena never mentioned her condition again. What she didn't realize was that a large percent of women who went west from the middle 1800s to early 1900s were in some stage of pregnancy. But things like that simply were not talked about.

That evening Tad and Matt related their trip to town and that supplies were just too expensive to purchase here. Then they offhandedly mentioned that Emma had run off some ruffians with the shotgun.

"What!" exclaimed Jasper. "We's olney gone a mite! Selena needed my hep down at the river."

"Well, let me tell you that I don't ever intend to just walk into camp while I know that Emma has that shotgun!" laughed Tad. Emma took the teasing good naturedly, but she also knew she had won their respect.

The incident also made them realize what a wild country they were traveling in and what precautions were to be observed from then on.

CHAPTER FOUR

The water level of the Neches had gone down in the last month, so traveling on the ferry across the river wasn't as dangerous as people had told them that it would be. Before the war, steamboat transportation of cotton was usually done between the months of December and May when the water levels were at their highest.

Tad and the others had to wait their turn as only two wagons and teams could fit on the ferry's platform at a time. Then the vessel had to return from the other side for another load.

They passed their time patiently like everyone else, enjoying the sight of a beautiful steamboat that had docked nearby. At night the lights of other campfires, fiddle music, and occasional singing made them somehow feel secure.

Finally it was time for their team and wagon. Seeing the size of the other Conestoga wagons, they realized that they were not very well equipped to travel several hundred miles across plains, mountains, and deserts.

Some had mules, others had oxen. And there seemed to be quite a dispute as to which type of animal was best for going west.

After crossing the Neches river, they passed by some Indian mounds. The locals told them that was where Indians had buried their dead a long time ago. Emma would have liked to have spent more time there, but no one else seemed very interested, so she didn't say anything.

The weather was just about perfect in the mornings. The trees offered shade in the afternoons, and the flowers along the way smelled heavenly. The bluebonnets had burned out long ago, but everywhere there were wildflowers of every color.

Crockett was the next town of any size they came to. They arrived in town just ahead of the stagecoach. Beautiful trees were planted around the town square, but the log courthouse had burned some months ago.

Jasper was surprised so many ex-slaves were in town. He discovered most of them still lived on the same plantations they had been on before the war, but now they were able to share in the crops. What they probably didn't realize was they would also have to share in the risks of farming.

Clapp's Ferry took them over the Trinity River. Packet boats were busy carrying supplies up and down the river along with soldiers going home. It cost them one dollar for the wagon and team to get on the ferry, ten cents for each rider on a horse, and five cents for anyone on foot.

It was fairly crowded at the ferry landing, but as they made their way away from the river, the noise subsided and an almost eerie feeling fell over the group.

The air was stifling hot and Emma felt she could hardly breathe. Not wanting to complain, she daintily dabbed at her neck and face with her handkerchief to keep the moisture from running down.

The light through the leaves and tall trees glowed with an almost surreal softness. The only sounds were those of the mules plodding along, the chains clanging together, and the wagon creaking over the rutted road.

Matt, Tad, and Jasper each laid a hand on their guns without saying a word of their feelings to the others. No one spoke, and all had become tensely aware of their surroundings. The women had started out walking, but when the men suggested they get back in the wagon, they got no arguments.

Noon came and went without their stopping. The women handed the men a slice of meat and bread that was left over from their last night's supper, and all just kept on a slow pace through the afternoon.

The feeling of tension finally subsided some, but all still kept a watchful eye out for anything unusual. The problem with Indians of any tribe was that they were artists at camouflage.

Dense oaks rose on both sides of the road leading on farther west. Making camp for the night was difficult because of the lack of room between the trees and travelers who continued on into the night. Small fires were built, although little sleep was to be found.

The next morning, Emma and Selena found the men talking to a man who looked for all the world like an old army scout. He was dressed in buckskins but wore army boots. His hat was of the western style with a wide brim, and a kerchief was tied loosely around his neck. A large hunting knife hung in a scabbard on his left side, while an army issue six-shooter hung on his right. His face, darkly tanned from much exposure to the elements, looked like a road map from squinting into the sun.

The men were talking in hushed tones, so the women tried hard not to look as if they were listening, even though they tried desperately to catch some of the words.

The men, finally speaking normally, invited the man to join them for some breakfast and coffee. Gladly accepting, he went to his saddlebag and got out his own cup.

Matt motioned to the man in the buckskin outfit, and continued introducing the women to him. "This is Scout Miller, from down south of here. He's been telling us to keep wary of any Indian sign, because they've been causing some problems around here."

"What kind of problems?" Emma asked with a raised eyebrow. The men knew they weren't going to get out of not telling more, so Matt decided to tell just what was needed.

"Just to the north of us yesterday, a young white girl was captured. Her family was killed and their place was burned. It appears that something has stirred the Indians up, and everyone traveling needs to be watchful."

When everyone was ready to move out, Scout Miller just naturally fell in with them. It appeared he was also headed toward San Antonio.

Madisonville was the next town. They passed by a beautiful log courthouse, a couple of general stores, a saloon, a school, and found themselves continuing on west.

Bedias Creek was the next watering hole for the animals. The women had planned to do some laundry at the next water they came to, but decided the water at this creek was too muddy from all of the travelers passing.

Fourteen miles on and they were making camp again at a place called Kurten's Farm. Several German families lived in the area and actually worked on the farm.

That evening they stayed in their first "wagon yard". They were told they would find these from time to time scattered along the Old San Antonio Road.

"Wagon yards" were places where early travelers could spend the night in comparable safety. It was usually an open area with stalls and feed rooms. Some were larger than others, and the travelers might even be charged for this convenience.

The family they were parked next to was anxiously waiting for other family members to arrive. They had become separated from each other at one of the ferries. With each new arriving group of wagons their concern was growing.

Scout Miller decided, without mentioning his concerns to anyone else, that if the missing wagon did not show up by morning, he would backtrack to see if they were in trouble.

There were twelve wagons parked in the area for the evening, and the aroma of coffee filled the air. Children were playing, women were sitting in small groups visiting, and the men were tending to the livestock and visiting among themselves.

Selena had just finished taking the Dutch oven she was baking biscuits in out of the coals, when a girl about the age of Emma came running into the wagon yard.

Out of breath, she quickly explained that her father had been burned and that they needed help. Looking in the direction she was pointing, they could see the glow of a fire.

By the time several of the men arrived at the farm it was obviously too late to save the barn. The injured man was able to tell them the fire started when a cow kicked over a lantern in the barn, but he was able to save all of the livestock.

Doc Turner did what he could, but the man's right arm was burned severely. The man's wife had some ointment, and they wrapped it carefully. Doc wished he could have done more. Most medicines were home remedies, and even they were pitifully few.

They spent most of the evening with the family, mainly so Doc could keep on eye on the injured man. Meanwhile Emma and the young lady became fast friends.

The German's had not heard that the War Between the States was over, but had guessed it by the number of soldiers returning to the area. Their men were either too old, or too young, but for the most part they did not want to get mixed up in the altercation.

The next morning Scout Miller noted the missing wagon had not come in. Unobserved, Tad Cummings watched Miller silently saddle his horse and steal away in the early morning light.

Dawn was barely breaking when Miller left camp to head back toward the Trinity River. When he neared Bedias Creek he found a burned wagon but no bodies and no mules. He found several tracks of unshod horses, and then picked up a faint trail of tracks. But these were boot tracks! He got down on one knee to examine them more closely. By the sizes and the indentions he could tell they were made by two men and a woman. One man was quite a bit heavier than the other.

Being a scout he knew a man walking will kick the grass down in the direction he's going, but a horse will kick the grass down in the direction from which it has come.

He continued to follow the tracks for about an hour. He found a place where they had all been on their knees, as if hiding, behind some scrub oaks. He saw places where they had stumbled, so he knew they were running part of the time.

The tracks were continuing on west, where the wagon camp had been the night before. Just before noon he spotted the three people. He gave them water, put the woman on his horse, and they made their way toward the wagon yard.

As they walked along they told how their wagon had been overcome by a war party of Comanche. The savages immediately seemed more interested in the mules than the people, which surprised them. Then the Indians started throwing things out of the wagon and discovered that liquor was there, as the family was hauling supplies to start a general store in California. It appeared to the family the Indians acted as if they were drunk already. They cut the harnesses and led the mules off, and after the bottles of liquor were passed around, they set fire to the wagon and were all gone as quickly as they had come. The family hid under some brush and was totally ignored.

Scout Miller laughed lightly at the story. "They probably were drunk on Mezcal. It's a drink made by the Mexicans out of a desert plant. Sometimes it was sold, or just given it to the Indians in trade for guns or captives. And more than likely they took your mules for meat. Indians would rather have mule meat than any other kind. You can actually be thankful they were already drunk, and a little sidetracked, or you wouldn't be here to tell this story!"

Introductions were finally made when they all arrived safely back at the wagon yard. The two heads of the families were brothers from Pennsylvania. One had a wife and two young children. The man who had just escaped certain death had his wife and son of eighteen with him. They would now have to travel the entire distance with the seven of them in one wagon. It would be crowded, but they were all relieved to be together again, and alive.

The next morning, the six were on their way again. The family of the burn victim had given them smoked meat and some of their wonderful German black bread to pay the doctor for his services. Making new friends and leaving them behind was very painful for Emma. She was not used to such brief friendships.

The city of Bryan came into view at about noon, a busy place that boasted of a railroad, a post office, and a telegraph. But they had hours to go before calling it a day. That evening was spent on the banks of the Brazos River. They would be one of the first in line the next morning for Moseley's Ferry.

Brazos River

Mosley's Ferry Crossing

That evening Scout Miller began to tell of some of his travels and experiences and had everyone within hearing distance spellbound. When one of the men from another wagon asked him where he was from, he smoothly sidestepped the question and continued with another exploit.

What the questioning man did not understand was that out west it was rude and sometimes dangerous to inquire where someone was from. Many secrets went west with men and women that they wanted to stay hidden.

Scout Miller ended his stories that night saying, "The early frontiersmen had a saying: "there was no Sunday west of St. Louis and no God west of Fort Smith." Everyone laughed and headed to their wagons for a little rest before traveling on the next day.

Caldwell was about 12 miles down the Old San Antonio Road. It was a beautiful little town, with hotels, a blacksmith shop, and several general stores. They all marveled at the beautiful red brick courthouse in the center of town.

Jasper noticed that one of the mules needed a new shoe and the wagon needed some attention. While the men tended to these things, the women went to one of the general stores for a small order of supplies.

Tensions about the war still ran high, and Selena and Emma walked into the middle of the conflict. A man dressed in Confederate grays pushed Selena aside with intentions of being waited on next. The only problem was that Jasper had seen the incident.

It was still a time when women were treated with utmost respect. It was considered deplorable for a woman to be mistreated. The war had been hard on women from both the North and the South. Atrocities had occurred on both sides, but it was still considered very wrong for a woman to be abused.

The women patiently waited for the boorish man to finish his business, and he left the store with a sneer on his face. He headed toward the back of the corrals where he had left his horse tied. While putting his supplies in his saddlebags, he noticed a large black man approaching him.

The size of the man made him catch his breath. Noticing that none of his friends (or anyone else for that matter) was within sight, he got a little more nervous.

Trying to sound brave, he asked in a rough tone, "What do you want, nigger?"

"I want chew to 'pologize to my wife," was the curt answer.

"What?" the man asked astounded. "I ain't goin' to do no such thang!" And he proceeded to take a swing at Jasper's chin.

Jasper merely ducked his head and chest back and reached over and slapped the arrogant man on top of his head. The man fell down at Jasper's feet as if dead.

Checking him to make sure he was still breathing, Jasper left the man to wake up with a terrible headache.

Jasper thought no one had witnessed the scene, but one person had observed the entire episode from the women in the store to the fight behind the corrals. Scout Miller missed very few comings and goings. He couldn't help but snicker to himself when Jasper knocked the man senseless. He decided Jasper was a man to ride the river with.

Miller walked on down to where the man was trying to stand up, reached down and handed him his hat. "If I were you, I'd head that-a-way," he said, pointing to the east. The poor man, still dazed, nodded feebly and staggered off.

Never having mentioning the incident to anyone, they left town the next morning heading farther westward.

They had now been traveling just over three weeks. Water had proven to be rather available, if they were careful. Wild meat had been abundant, but they had to take care not to get the attention of other wild things, such as the Comanche!

The next day promised to be another hot, sweaty day, but by noon the sky was telling another story. Storm clouds had come from nowhere, and the wind was starting to howl.

Within the hour the men decided it was best to make camp early. A short, winding trail took them up to a small cave on the side of a hill that faced east. The wind was blowing from the west, so they were completely out of the wind. It was a struggle to coax the animals up the incline, but once there, grass was pulled for them and they became less frightened. The little wagon was left down below in a protected area.

The men went to work chopping wood so they could stay comfortable. There is something about having a fire blazing that is a comfort to people. They could all tell it was going to be quite a storm.

Supplies were brought up from the wagon, and the women began making coffee and stew. Selena added some wild onions to the stew, and the aroma made everyone forget how miserable it was outside.

Jasper disappeared once more and came back carrying the small wooden chest. "What's that?" asked Captain Cummings. Jasper opened the top and showed him the papers that were inside. "Aw can't read, but Miss Emma tole us dey was impotant papers and to gib um to her daddy when we seen him. Sompine bout deeds to de land."

Tad and Matt shared a knowing look, but didn't try to explain anything at this time. The papers consisted of plantation records of crop sales, overseer's reports, and accounts.

By late afternoon the sky had grown to an ugly gray-green color, and the clouds were huge and low. Everyone was grateful to be in the cave when the rains came and the wind howled even harder.

It got dark early that evening. Emma was glad to have her grandmother's quilts with her, as they were very warm, and well made. She hated to see them on the ground, but somehow she knew Grandmother would understand. Then she noticed the little chest sitting on a rock in the corner. "Oh, you brought it up! Thank you, Jasper," she exclaimed, as she bent over and set it in her lap.

Opening the lid, a sheepish grin came to her lips. Suddenly she was holding the entire shelf in her hand, and was looking down into the bottom of the chest. Everyone instinctively leaned over Emma's shoulder and peered down. There were six $50 gold coins, each resting in its own carved out niche. On top of these was a small velvet jewelry bag. Emma untied the string at the top and into her hand tumbled her Grandmother's string of pearls. She held them to herself for a moment, and then gently let them slide back into the bag.

"As you see, the chest has a false bottom," she unnecessarily explained. Everyone was still staring at the gold coins. "Ah never seen so much money 'fo," Jasper finally whispered. "I have, but it has sure been awhile," added Doc Turner.

"This is what Grandfather meant when he said it would help us on our journey," Emma went on to explain. "Our grandparents intended to give these gold coins to my sister and me as wedding gifts."

"Wedding gifts?" asked Doc Turner surprised. "You were engaged to be married?"

"No, not yet, this was to be my dowry," giggled Emma. "But I fear that it may be desperately needed to help us just survive this journey."

"That's pretty mature thinking for a kid," Captain Cummings commented while pouring another cup of coffee. "I had been thinking since none of us had any money, we would have to stop and work for a while at the next town of any size. Jasper and I could do some blacksmithing, and of course, Doc Turner could practice his voodoo. But all of that would put us months behind in getting to California."

"Will three hundred dollars in gold even be enough?" asked Doc Turner, mainly turning to Captain Cummings. "I don't think this little wagon is going to be sturdy enough for the entire way, and these mules have definitely seen better days. How much would it cost to outfit just our little band? I've noticed Jasper has a shotgun. I only carry a revolver, and you have one, and there's a couple of Bowie knives between us, and as far as I've seen, that's it!"

"Well, let's just take stock of things, since we are talking. We're three men, with two women along with us, in the middle of Indian and comanchero country, with five weapons among us. Probably the safest thing to do would be sign up with a wagon train. We'll probably be seeing some on the road."

The debris from the storm was strewn about for miles! Thick tree trunks and limbs were everywhere. The men went in front of the wagon removing obstacles too big to go around. They only made about twelve miles the first day after the storm.

The next two days they rolled along on the well- traveled road meeting several freighters, and trailing behind other wagons much like theirs, headed for San Antonio. The huge freighters were obviously loaded with supplies of one kind or another, and a few would probably end up as far-east as New Orleans.

The group made their way over two small creeks, passed some farms, and rather enjoyed the lovely rolling hills. Had it not been for the fact that Emma needed to be reunited with her father, all would have been tempted to stay longer in such a peaceful place.

For all of the beauty around them, they were continually reminded of how destitute Texas had become during the last years of the war. It was still too early for the gardens to have much produce, and only a few sheep and cattle dotted the landscape. Occasionally a lone rooster would let his presence be known, and the only ducks to be seen were wild ones on small ponds.

One thing notably missing to Jasper and Selena was that they had seen no blacks working in the fields for many miles now. This area had been settled by the German immigrants for about 40 years. Even as poor as the war had left everyone, their homesteads were still neat and clean. But no sign of any slaves was to be seen.

As Bastrop came into view, they were surprised to see the charred remains of burned-out buildings. Almost the entire downtown area was gone. Assuming it had happened from the war, they learned

Bastrop had not been invaded by the Yankees, but that arson had been blamed.

Nothing fresh could be purchased here, as the town had only begun to start rebuilding. With all of the men off to war, there was no one to start the reconstruction of the town.

This area was a place early settlers had come to for protection when the Indians decided to raid. This had also been a hunting ground for the Comanche every fall for a good many years.

They began meeting teams of oxen hauling logs out of a nearby forest. Industry was beginning again, and a people with little hope were starting over. At a couple of places their wagon was actually forced to leave the road so that the huge lumber wagons with eight iron-rimmed wheels could continue on.

Sightings of Tarbox & Brown stagecoaches were becoming more frequent on the road as they came nearer the town of San Marcos. They camped early that evening because the women wanted time to enjoy the warm springs that were nearby. Selena and Emma giggled and splashed each other in the sheer delight at being able to soak in the spring water.

The men left Doc Turner to watch the team and keep an eye on the women playing in the water, and went into town to catch up on any news. The saloons were usually the best place for this, so that's where they headed. Jasper was very nervous about being in crowds of white men, but Tad told him to just follow him. Everyone just assumed Jasper had been Tad's slave, and looked the other way.

Scout Miller was more at home than the others in this territory, and knew how to get information quickly. More stories of Indian uprisings all the way to California were what they kept hearing. Most of the forts were insisting on military escorts for anyone going west.

Arriving back at camp, they found Doc Turner had been talked into helping Emma wash her hair. He was pouring a pitcher of the warm spring water over her long hair as the men walked up. Tad stood with arms crossed and looked on with a teasing grin on his face. Matt turned red down to his collar.

He quickly handed Emma the towel she had laid to one side and began asking questions about what they had found out in town.

"We heard more bad news about Indians being on the warpath. I guess miners and white settlers have them all riled up. It sounds like we'll probably have to have soldiers escort us all the way to California."

That evening after supper they all took note of the Doc and Emma's walking off a safe distance, and talking in the moonlight. It was becoming clear to everyone that a romance was blooming.

Jasper and Selena were very uncomfortable with this new behavior from Emma. They both liked Doc Turner, but Emma was their responsibility until she could be handed over to her father.

The pretty town of New Braunfels was easily reached by the next day around noon. This was one of the largest communities in Texas. They passed by several general stores, a blacksmith, two saloons, a sawmill, and even a store that sold soap and candles.

Here again, life was just barely existing. But one thing the group kept seeing was the hope in people's eyes. Some of the people they visited with were not even aware the war was over. News about the war in the east had not caught up here in Texas yet.

Most of the families who were in town were of German descent. They apparently settled in this area about twenty or thirty years ago. A main source of income was sheep's wool, while another was the beautiful furniture they built from the lumber of a nearby forest.

Emma and Selena stood on a wooden sidewalk and peered through a window at the beautiful household furniture displayed there. Big massive beds, dressers, dining tables of every size, and beautiful rocking chairs seemed to be looking back at them.

Emma could only dream right now of keeping house with such beautiful furnishings, but she was hoping that her time was coming soon. She found herself growing fonder of Matt Turner every day.

Selena, having never owned any fine furniture, found herself only admiring the beautiful shiny wood that was gleaming like glass.

Neither of them had any intentions of going inside such an elaborate store, and eventually moved on down the street to gaze into a dress shop where women's hats were beautifully displayed in the front window.

Emma remembered going shopping with her grandmother and never thinking a thing about buying at least two dresses, with bonnets to match, on each trip. Sometimes her grandmother would purchase fabric and then spend days sewing dresses for special occasions for her and Lena.

A feeling of melancholy slipped over Emma and, try as she might, she couldn't shake it. Things had happened too quickly, and now the excitement of the trip to see her father had almost turned to pure fear. Getting to be reunited with her father was feeling more and more like a distant dream that might never happen.

Selena sensed Emma's depression, and began giving her orders for the first time of tasks needing to be done. She knew from her own experiences in life that the way to overcome fear and depression was to stay busy.

Living outdoors the way they were meant that everyone had to work to make it pleasant. Wood needed to be gathered, chopped, and fires had to be built. Water was a constant source of worry, and everyone had to be frugal with it.

Within a couple of days, Emma's good humor had returned, and to the delight of everyone she began acting like her old self. They had made it safely all the way to San Antonio, and for some reason they all felt a great deal of relief.

The wagon yard was near Military Plaza, which was down the street from Alamo Plaza. Tad and Matt decided to buy some new clothes, because all they had were confederate grays. Times were hard enough without drawing undue attention to your self.

They all enjoyed visiting the mission on the Alamo Plaza and hearing the details of the famous battle that had taken place here between the Texans and the Mexicans many years back. There was a thick stone and adobe wall enclosing the plaza. The military now rented the mission chapel as a supply depot.

A nice park was constructed around the Plaza, and people were busy coming and going in wagon trains from all directions. There were even some arriving from Chihuahua City, as San Antonio lay on the trade route with Mexico.

Scout Miller once again mingled with soldiers and freighters and reported the news to the group. The commander of the garrison insisted all travelers going west or east have an escort. News of a surveyor being scalped by the Comanche near Austin had put everyone on the alert more than ever.

The group realized this was the road they had just come over! Maybe all of the Indian activity was why they had felt such an uneasy feeling for several days through that part of the country. Whatever the reason, they all realized how lucky they had been not to have run into any of the warriors.

A military escort of six soldiers took them west out of San Antonio toward Fort Inge outside Uvalde.

Castroville was the first small community they came to after crossing the Leon River. Here they came across houses which were stark white because of the white washed mortar plastered over adobe. Most of the residents were of German and French heritage.

Emma began to notice that their surroundings had begun to take on a totally different appearance. They were encountering more desert plants, and purple mountains could be seen in the distance. The days were getting hotter, and the sun beat down on them unmercifully.

Selena and Emma began to always wear bonnets to help shade their faces. Each of the men from the beginning of the trip had worn a hat. Wide-brimmed hats were a must when they were out in the searing sun.

The little town of D'Hanis, a French settlement built on the Seco River, came and went quickly.

Camp Sabinal, on the Sabinal Creek, was a busy mud hole where several travelers were stopped until proper escort could get them on to Uvalde. There were several Union officers there, as well as some Texas Rangers. The six cavalrymen decided they could take on one more wagon. The family who had been waiting the longest quickly gathered things together and joined the group.

They arrived at Fort Inge, built near the town of Uvalde, mid-morning of the next day. Two more wagons of traveler's awaited escort, so six more soldiers were detached to join them on the trail to Fort Clark.

They were told they would be leaving in two days. Scout Miller was the most outspoken against the added delay, but a little rest sounded wonderful to the girls.

CHAPTER FIVE

The forts along the lower road were originally spaced so that a horse and rider could go from one fort to the next in the span of one day. Wagons with teams were, of course, another story. The roads were usually two narrow ruts going over rough, rocky, uneven ground. Twenty miles a day was usually unheard of, but a distance of twelve miles was fairly common.

The road they now traveled was the Butterfield Overland Mail Route used for the San Antonio-San Diego route. Stage stations were placed along the way for travelers and freighters going west.

This route was a mere 2,800 mile trip through some of the most desolate country on the continent. When Mr. John Butterfield was awarded the government contract in 1857, he decided the stagecoaches should be able to do this trip in 25 days. What he did not account for was the future encounters with an embittered Apache chief Cochise!

Cochise and Mangas Colorado (or Red Sleeves) were both Apache chiefs. The name "Apache" actually referred to several different tribes or bands. Cochise was member of the Chiricahua tribe, while Mangas Colorado (sometimes spelled Coloradas) was a member of the Mimbreno tribe. Some of the larger better known Apache tribes in New Mexico and Arizona were the Mescalero, the White Mountain, and the Jicarilla.

During their earlier years they were inclined to pretty much ignore the "white eyes" who passed through their part of the country. Many white men even lived peacefully with the Indians.

But in 1860, some very foolish miners from Pinos Altos took Mangas Colorado hostage, tied him to a tree, and proceeded to horsewhip him into telling them where the Apache "big gold mine" was. Of course, there was no gold mine. But there were plenty of Apaches around to take reprisal for this act! It was estimated some 100 people were killed by Indian attacks by the end of 1862.

They parked the wagon with the others near the bank of the Leona River. That evening singing could be heard, and occasionally music from a fiddle or a harmonica could be enjoyed.

The women were grateful for a couple of days respite. Jasper immediately dug a small fire pit and started a fire so there would be hot coals for Selena to cook with the Dutch ovens. She usually used two, one for meat and the other for bread. She even stacked them sometimes.

One of the local products was some wonderful honey, and Selena outdid herself making biscuits and serving them hot with some of the honey.

The men decided that if a fresher team of mules could be found it would be a good idea to switch mules before going on farther.

The ones they had were those that Jasper had started out with from the plantation. They all decided to trade off the smaller wagon for a larger one with a double thick cover over it. Furthermore, they needed to add two Sharps carbines to their arsenal. They hoped all this could be found at Fort Clark.

The days were getting hotter, and the terrain was becoming very sparse. The beautiful, big live oak trees that had shaded the trail for so long were becoming a thing of the past.

Fort Clark was a good two to three days journey, but water would be available. The road continued to be well-traveled and almost smooth in places. They could see the Turkey Mountains off in the distance to the right. The Nueces River proved easy to cross this time of year as the water level was very low.

A thin layer of dust began to settle on everything. A slow realization that the sand and dust would probably get worse before it got better began to dawn on most of the travelers.

A lovely grove of big oak trees lining the Moras River was their first view of Fort Clark. Women were washing clothes and hanging them to dry on the bushes near the bank. Soldiers were filling water barrels on small carts, while the horses stood knee deep in the spring.

Coming around the parade ground, they could see one of the barracks had been burned, and the flag pole in the center was broken in half.

The story told them was that in 1861 Federal troops were to surrender the fort over to the Confederates, but on leaving they broke the flag pole so the Confederate flag could not be flown and in retaliation set fire to barracks and other buildings on their departure.

The military escort felt relief no Indian sign had been seen, and reported such to the commander. The frontier soldiers that had been stationed there for months laughed at them and said, "Don't you believe it! Just because you didn't see them, don't mean a thang out here! They was watch'n you every step of the way!"

All in all it felt like an oasis in the desert. The fort was all they had hoped it would be. The sutler's store had fresh vegetables, a fresh team of mules was there for the trading, and the men were able to pick up the firearms they had wanted.

Another escort was heading out toward Fort Lancaster the next morning, and there was room for one more wagon. There would be five wagons, with 18 cavalrymen and a military ambulance to pick up a colonel coming from Fort Bowie.

But before reaching Fort Lancaster, which was still over a hundred and seventy miles away, Fort Hudson was their next goal. It was only seventy-five miles away, and through some of the worse Indian territory they had been in yet!

Along the way they met Mexican caravans selling their produce and wares. Most of the travelers were stopping for the day by two or three o'clock in the afternoon and traveling in the cool of the evening and early morning.

The water stops were averaging 10 to 12 miles apart. They had such names as Turkey Creek, Maveric Creek, and Painted Caves.

Destiny Road

Fort Hudson was located on San Pedro Creek, a tributary of the Devil's River. The walls of the buildings were constructed of a mixture of gravel and lime. This made the buildings cool in the summer and warm in the winter. Even a post office had been established there.

Camp Hudson Monument

Sitting around the fires that night, tales of a camel caravan passing through in 1859 were told. It seems a fellow by the name of Beale was experimenting with camels in the Southwest. He was sure they would do better and go farther than oxen and mules. He was hoping the military would agree with him and that he could supply them with the camels. But it turned out the camels had two real problems. First, they had a terrible odor; and secondly, the horses were scared to death of them. Unfortunately, the War Between the States came in 1861, and the experiment became a failure. Most of the camels were simply released to roam free.

It was still a good six or seven days from Fort Lancaster when the group started out the next day. Once again a strong feeling of restlessness began to overcome them, and everyone was warned to keep a sharp lookout for Indians.

One of the cavalrymen exclaimed, "The air feels like Injuns!" Tad and the others had not had any experience with Indian fighting yet, but they knew enough to stay prepared. The women in the wagons were told to load all pistols and keep ammunition ready.

It was hot, and the only air to breathe was filled with the dust stirred up by the horses and wagons as they plodding along. No one spoke, and everyone was looked forward to the small spring that was coming into view.

The women had long ago put away the many petticoats they had once thought of as a necessity. Common sense and practicality had taken over several hundred miles back.

Each was in his own thoughts when a fearful noise seemed to come right up out of the ground! The first two soldiers riding point were the first to fall from their horses. Wild yells surrounded the train, and smoke and gunshots added to the terrifying confusion.

Jasper had one of the new Sharps, and immediately put it to use. Tad was busy on his own end, but noticed what a good shot Jasper was and how he kept a cool head during the thick of the battle. He realized how valuable that would be on this dangerous passage west.

Selena and Emma each held a pistol pointed toward the back of the wagon. Suddenly the noise was gone, and the silence was deafening. Doc Turner stuck his head into the wagon to check on the women and then went to see about the wounded. The soldiers quickly brought the wagons around into a circle and prepared for another attack. They didn't have long to wait.

The Indians were slightly outnumbered and were definitely outgunned. With the second attack, the Indians lost too many braves and retreated.

The soldiers had lost two good men and two others had been wounded. Doc Turner was once again needed on the battlefield, and he wondered if life could ever be normal again. The only difference this time was that he had a pretty assistant by his side.

The group finally limped into Fort Lancaster and found local Mexican families living in the area but the fort deserted. Several forts had been abandoned during the war, and this was causing the Indians to grow braver.

Fort Lancaster Ruins

One of the families shared a roasted goat with them that evening and told them stories of the Indians and Comancheros.

Comancheros were a group of traders that apparently had a special relationship with the Comanche. They traded guns and other supplies with Indians and ranchers alike, but they also had a dark side to them. They also dealt in the trading and ransoming of captives and slaves all the way from Mexico to the Panhandle of Texas. Most settlers feared the Comancheros almost as much as they feared the Comanche.

The Mexican family at Fort Lancaster warned them about leaving their livestock and women unattended. They spoke of Jose Tafoya, a well known comanchero, who was especially feared in those parts.

At the mention of Tafoya's name, Scout Miller's head turned quickly to the speaker. "Do you think he's still in the area?"

The old man who was head of the house laughed loudly as he said, "I know he is, he stole some horses from me just two nights ago right out from under my nose!"

The next morning before leaving, Selena and Emma walked over to the fort cemetery and put flowers on two children's graves that they had seen earlier. Someone several years ago had lovingly hand carved the headstones.

One read ARTHUR TRACY LEE; DIED 9 JULY 1857; AGE 15 MONTHS. The other simply said LITTLE MARGARET; DIED 13 OCT. 1858.

Children's Gravestones in Ft. Lancaster Cemetery

Soldier's Gravestone also in Ft. Lancaster Cemetery

Both women stood silently for a few moments looking at the little graves. Each thought of how hard it would have been to bury children and then have to move on without them. They were blissfully unaware that hundreds of such graves littered all of the trails and roads leading west.

The Pecos River crossing was too swollen from recent rains in the mountains, so they were delayed on its banks for two days. Everyone kept a watchful eye out, and no one was allowed to wander off alone.

Pecos River

Several days later they made it to Comanche Springs (later known as Fort Stockton). A long flat mesa was to their right, and a strange looking pointed hill lay to their left, all formed and shaped by the almost never ending wind. Supplies had begun to run short, but water was still in abundance. The spring was a good place to camp except for the scarcity of wood. The open prairie allowed for good visibility of dust from anyone approaching for miles around.

Emma thought it unusual that the days were hot and the evenings so cool. While spreading her bed under the wagon one evening, the noise of horses galloping into the camp made her jump behind a wheel to try to hide.

Selena was at the campfire with the coffee pot in her hand. Jasper was sitting on a water barrel mending a harness. Tad and Matt were standing in the middle of the campsite, each with a coffee cup in his left hand, their right hands trying desperately to stay away from their guns until they could figure out who was coming up in such a rush.

When the dust had cleared, three Mexican men were sitting on the most beautiful horses that any of them had seen in this part of the country. Their saddles had silver concho decorations, as did the men's boots and jackets. Their hats were of the enormous sombrero style, and their spurs had large rowels.

The man in the middle was the oldest of the three and did all of the talking. "I see you have coffee made. May we join your fire?" he asked in a strong Mexican accent.

Tad had become the spokesman for the group some time back, so he answered now with a nod of his head, "Get on down". The rest of the group tried to act as normal as possible, knowing immediately that these men had to be comancheros, and very likely were the ones the man a few nights back had warned them about.

They did not leave him wondering for long. "My name is Jose Tafoya, and these are two of my riders," he said with an elegant sweep of his large hat.

Tad made short introductions around the camp, and for the first time realized that Scout Miller had disappeared. Small talk resumed as coffee was poured, but the men remained cautious and gave no information about their travel plans.

After a short period of time the Mexican men thanked Selena for the coffee with a "Gracias Senora", and began saying good-bye.

After mounting their horses, Jose turned to Tad with a jovial smile and said, "We have observed your group for several days and you have some good fighting men with you." He nodded in Jasper's direction. "This is very dangerous country you travel in. Be very careful. Friends can be useful!" he added before spurring his horse into action. They were gone as quickly as they had come.

"What do you think of that!" exclaimed Matt still shocked. A voice behind them calmly stated, "I think you made a friend."

Tad turned to see Scout Miller ambling up with his cup in his hand, and nonchalantly poured himself a cup of coffee. "Now you show up!" was the teasing reply.

"That was Jose's way of telling you his men will protect you while we're in his territory," Miller explained. "For some reason he has taken a liking to your group."

The soldier escort camped nearby had been closely observing the visitors but were too far away to hear the conversations. Major Dunson came over in disbelief that the well-known comanchero had dared to pay this particular group a friendly visit.

"Do you know who that was?" he asked incredulously.

"Yep! He introduced himself!" Tad answered with a laugh.

"Well, he'll bear watching!" was the tart remark.

A couple of nights after leaving Comanche Springs, Major Dunson of the cavalry, announced that they were to have a cold camp

Destiny Road

that night. No fires or lights of any kind were allowed. Two of the scouts had seen Indian signs for several miles, and he saw no reason to let the Indians know their exact location.

Scout Miller had been going out with the scouts for days at a time. Although Emma and Selena didn't know him very well at all, they always felt a sigh of relief when he rode back in. They instinctively knew that he was a man they could depend on in Indian territory.

While he was gone, the other five spoke out loud about him and wondered about his past life and where he had acquired the name of "Scout". They began to realize they really didn't know very much about him, but they were all very aware they desperately needed him.

The scouts came back to report that Fort Davis had recently been abandoned by the Union troops and that several Mexican families were living within the walls of the fort. This was discouraging news for the soldiers who wondered why they had not been told of this before leaving Fort Clark. They then realized the telegraph wires had probably been torn down by the Indians, and with the war in the East just ending, there were not enough soldiers to man the entire southwest.

Fort Davis lay off to the southwest in what was known as the Davis Mountains. No one had to be told to be on the alert, for the "feeling that makes the hair stand up on the back of yore neck" was everywhere. They knew they were being watched, but couldn't see a real sign anywhere. When Apaches don't want to be seen, they're not!

Cold camps were getting to be a normal occurrence by the time they pulled into Fort Davis. Sure enough, several Mexican families were using the facilities as home, and several hard-looking men were also hanging around.

Fort Davis

These were the ones that worried the soldiers the most. It was a known fact that outlaws hung out in these mountains, and with the military pulling out, it was a heyday for them. The only option now was to go on to Fort Bliss at El Paso, because they had come too far to turn back.

They were again asked by several of the families to stay for a meal, as they always wanted to hear of news and share information. But, this time, they felt it best that they just moved on. The women were even quieter than usual, and made sure they kept their heads and faces covered with scarves. They were all relieved when they left the fort.

The scouts took turns all afternoon back tracking their trail to see if they were being followed. Sure enough, just before dusk, Captain Cummings spotted a puff of dust about a quarter of a mile back.

"We're going to set up a dummy camp," Major Dunson whispered. "We'll not even take time for coffee but make them think we're settling down for the night. We used this trick more than once during the war."

Of course, it could just be another traveler, but in this country you couldn't afford to assume. By morning they were miles ahead of where they were thought to be.

Seventy miles in hostile country can be a long, long way. They found some game for meat along the way. Antelope and rabbit were plentiful. Jasper and Matt were the main meat providers. They made sure no ammunition was wasted.

Chihuahuan Desert Country

Selena and Emma were becoming quite a team at the camp chores. Emma had learned how to make coffee, and was quite proud of herself. Selena had also taught her how to bake biscuits, and to make stews from practically anything!

The Rio Grande had almost no fish and was only about three feet deep in most places. They had been able to purchase a small amount of garden produce at a small rancho they had stopped at.

They were two days out, and the feeling that things were not quite right came over the group again.

Road to Fort Quitman

They moved on as silently as mules and wagons can, and kept a watchful eye out.

The Rio Grande was always to their left, and a small mountain range lay to their right. The terrain was fairly desolate with various desert plants dotting the scenery. It was hot, dry and dusty. A fine white coat of dust seemed to lie on everything.

Strangers in this part of the country could mean anything, but they usually meant trouble. About mid-morning on the third day out, three strangers came galloping up to the group just as they were approaching a watering place called Deadman's Hole.

Tad Cummings and Matt Turner recognized them immediately as the hard cases they had seen way back at Fort Davis. Fortunately, so did Major Dunson and his men.

Major Dunson did the talking for the group. "Good morning, how can we be of service?"

The men pretended to begin conversation, but one suddenly drew his pistol and fired it into the nearest soldier. As all guns were immediately drawn and shots filled the air, a thunderous roar of more horsemen came from over a hill to their right. The wagons were pulled into a circle as quickly as possible, but the sudden fighting had taken them all by surprise. They had been teaching all of the women how to load guns and how to fire them. Their efforts were about to pay off.

The outlaws quickly realized they were badly outnumbered, and out-gunned!

Suddenly, one of the young girls started to run across the compound to the aide of her father who had been wounded. One of the outlaws charged in, scooped her up on his saddle with him and rode away into the dust and gun-smoke, leaving her mother screaming hysterically behind them.

As suddenly as the outlaws had come, they were gone. Only the eerie sound of the mother's sobs and of guns being reloaded remained.

Five men of the caravan had been killed. Two were soldiers, the others from the wagons. Several more were wounded, some more seriously than others, as well as one of the women. Although Doc Turner was the only doctor in the group, several were tending to those with minor wounds.

Major Dunson had only two scouts to spare to go looking for the girl. Scout Miller volunteered to go with them. Being this close to Mexico, captives were usually sold to Comancheros, but if they could rescue her before crossing the Rio Grande ... It was only hopeful thinking.

The scouts decided to go in different directions for the rescue attempt. While Scout Miller went west, one went north, and the other southeast.

The road to Van Horn Wells was well known for Indian attacks. Many settlers had tried to farm and ranch in the area, but most had been killed or driven out by the Apaches.

The stagecoach lines and freighters dreaded these mountain roads because of the numerous spots that were well known for ambush.

One of the families who were traveling with them since leaving San Antonio was the Joel Johnson family. Mr. and Mrs. Johnson were in their late thirties, and their daughter was eleven years old. Emma had enjoyed traveling and visiting with this family in particular because they reminded her so of her parents and family.

The Johnson's came from Springfield, Missouri, and Van Horn Wells was their end destination. Mr. Johnson carried with him a letter of employment at the Hazel Mine. This mine was one of the top producers of silver in the country.

Destiny Road

An early settler of the area, Thomas Owen, had opened the mine back in 1856. But, after four years of war and constant attacks from the Mescalero Apache, Mr. Owen was forced to abandon work at the mine.

After arriving at Van Horn Wells the Johnson's were crushed to discover that his letter of intended employment was useless. They now had to rethink their plans for the future.

A Major Jefferson Van Horne had reportedly discovered the water wells in 1849, near the present town site. It had become a mail route stop on the San Antonio-San Diego road.

Having nothing to return to Missouri for, and no hopes of work at this present location, the Johnson family had no real options except to keep traveling on with the wagon train. They would be among the throngs of people who hoped for better opportunities in the west.

One of the first things Major Dunson did upon his arrival was send a telegram to Fort Bliss, which was near El Paso, and describe briefly the girl's capture. He was hoping to alert the fort to be on the look-out for comanchero and outlaw activity in their area. Through concerted efforts occasionally captives were found.

The other travelers continued to be sympathetic to the family, and tried in many ways to make their loss less painful. They kept encouraging them with stories they had heard about captives being found and returned to their families, and reminding them of the scouts out searching for her.

But the mother was not to be consoled. They had started on this trip from South Carolina. Her husband had been headstrong in going west for a new start, and she had no choice but to follow. Their youngest child had died of a fever just after getting into Texas. She told of how hard it was to leave that little grave, but the other wagons had held up for two days already on account of their sick child, and were ready to move on. She thought her burden was already more than she could bear, and now this.

Jenny was only nine years old. Her mother held onto a favorite doll which had been the girls, and as the days passed she became more and more silent.

They remained at Van Horn Wells for two days. After refilling water barrels, and resting some, they were ready to journey on into the desert.

Fort Quitman could be reached in about seven days. It was August, 1865.

CHAPTER SIX

Scout Miller approached the water hole with caution. He had lived too long in this country to be foolish. He had seen nothing, but that only made him more wary. He circled the rocks almost soundlessly. He had learned to watch his horses' ears in times like this. If they twitched back and forth there was another animal nearby, but if they were pitched forward it was a man.

The horse was standing stock still with both ears pitched forward and starring at a bunch of manzanita bushes!

No one west of the Mississippi ever questioned a man's name, or asked too many questions about his past. So it was with Scout Miller. That was all anyone ever called him, but he carried a story like so many other men.

When Miller came west before the war, he was a hunted man. Having been convicted of a crime he never committed, he could not even convince his own family of his innocence. Disgusted and angry, he fled west. When the war came, he joined the cavalry and was lost on the Frontier. Like so many, he assumed a new identity, a new life, and never looked back.

That had been a forever ago. Now the war was over, and so was his commission in the cavalry. He had grown to love the West, and, in a strange way, to understand its inhabitants some. He had dealings with the Comanche, Comancheros, and the Apache. And he trusted none of them.

He had started west for the gold fields he had heard so much about, but for now it had been his good luck to team up with the little group he had helped out. They needed him as much as he needed them.

He didn't have gold fever like so many. He was just going for the adventure. And west was definitely better than east. But first he had to get across Texas, New Mexico Territory, and Arizona Territory, which in 1865 was no easy feat. Not to mention there were "unfriendlies" everywhere! Then you had to deal with the desert, the sun, the wind, and the rattlesnakes, and the fact that there was no water in some areas for miles! And he hadn't even reached Fort Bliss yet.

Water meant life out in these desolate areas. The Rio Grande would be on their left all the way to Fort Quitman and on to Fort Bliss. He was now traveling through the Quitman Mountains.

He continued to scout ahead of the Wagon Train, always keeping a close eye out for any sign of the captured girl. He had left the other scouts several hours ago, and was on his own, just the way he liked it.

The area was covered with manzanita bushes, cholla, and gama grass. The grass was particularly tall and thick at the edge of the water hole. On Miller's right-hand side was a rock cliff about 50 feet high.

While his horse continued to stare in the direction of the water hole, he dismounted as quickly and soundlessly as possible. As he inched forward, a patch of red cloth came to view out of the corner of his eye. He tried not to stare. Men tend to develop a "sixth sense" when stared at. He inched forward a little more. No movement came from the direction of the red cloth.

He was now close enough to see a patch of red cloth tied around the forehead of a Mexican woman, and probably one of the most beautiful women he had ever seen! Her black hair was lying loose around her soft curved shoulders. Her soft, smooth olive skin seemed to be slightly blushed, possibly even feverish. As he reached out to put his hand on her forehead, she spoke so suddenly that he nearly fell backwards!

"Help me!" came the mumbled words in Spanish. Miller had always claimed that he knew just enough Spanish to get him into trouble. Well, here it was!

"Here, take a drink. You're burning up with fever", Scout Miller replied while unscrewing the top off his canteen that hung by his side. The woman could hardly swallow, but tried to do so with all the grace she could muster at the time. " *Now here is a lady*," thought Miller to himself.

Over the course of the next few moments, Miller dipped her red cloth in water several times and went from her forehead to dabbing a little all over her face. He offered her another drink, and felt she was recovering somewhat.

She finally spoke again with a faint "Gracias, Senor."

"Who are you? And how in the world did you get here?" Miller asked softly, more to himself than to the woman.

For most of the afternoon he tended to the injured woman. She seemed to be resting comfortably on a pallet he made for her, so he went on about the business of setting up camp and building a fire.

He fried some bacon and opened a can of beans, and was pouring himself a cup of coffee, when she surprised him by speaking in English. "The food smells wonderful!"

He turned to see her sitting up and watching him. He suddenly felt terribly uncomfortable. He was not used to having other people watch him so closely, especially such a pretty woman as this one.

He fixed her a plate of food and was handed her a cup of coffee. "Who are you, and what are you doing here?" he asked again.

She began to tell him her story. "I was taken captive by the Comancheros from my village in Sonora. I was sold to the Apaches in the mountains and became a wife to one of the chiefs. I lived there two years, and then the Comancheros came to reclaim me, saying my family was paying a big reward for me. There was a big fight, and my husband was killed in the battle. In the end I was forced to go with the Comancheros. I knew they were lying about my family's paying for me. We were very poor people. I had no idea where we were going, but I knew I had to get away. Then one night a group of Mexican soldiers came riding into camp. I discovered that these

Destiny Road

soldiers were not true to our country, but only highway robbers like the Comancheros. Then I recognized one of them! It was Pedro Rodriguez from our village. He was riding with them. He came over with his plate for me to serve him more frijoles, and spoke so low I could only catch a few words. But I understood "Watch me, and be ready."

"During the evening he arose, and went to his horse, pretending to take a guard post out near some rocks. He didn't even look in my direction, but rode away. In about an hour's time he was back and went to the fire for coffee. He still had his horse's reins in his hand when, suddenly, he grabbed my wrist, jumped on his horse's back and pulled me up behind him. I thought my arm was broken! It happened so quickly that it took the men in camp a minute to rally their thoughts. But by then we were already speeding across the desert.

"All I knew was that we were heading south. Then there were shots from the dark, and Pedro fell from the horse. As low as I could, I rode away in the night. My right arm was hurting something terrible, but I could not stop. I remember falling from the horse and hitting my head, then the next thing I saw you here helping me."

She finally finished her story and the food. She quietly thanked him and then lay back down and was immediately asleep again.

"Well," thought Scout Miller, "Here I am with a captive woman being chased by the Comancheros, and all I was worried about were Indians and water!" he laughed to himself. He laid his rough hand as gently as he knew how on her forehead to check to see if the fever was still there. She was still warm, but not as hot as when he had first found her.

He covered her with his blanket, stoked the fire, and lay down on his bedroll nearby. He slept light all night, checked her frequently, and kept a small fire going.

He rose early and was fixing coffee when she awoke and suddenly asked him, "Do you think my horse is still nearby?"

He doubted it, but promised her that after breakfast he would check the area. She seemed to have regained some strength and appetite. As they ate, an easy companionship seemed to fall between them and he began telling her something about himself. Suddenly he heard his horse whinny. He paused, waiting. Another horse nearby answered it.

He immediately went in search of the missing horse and found it some small distance away, chomping contentedly on gama grass. After resting a little while longer, he explained to the woman they needed to be moving, and that Fort Quitman was not far away.

He considered tying the woman on her saddle, but decided against it, when he saw that she was apparently able to ride.

Toward dusk they entered what had been Fort Quitman. It looked like a ghost town. The only light showing was through the window of an old adobe building in a poor state of repair.

He helped the woman off her mount, and she fell into his arms. He carried her up the steps and kicked at the door a couple of times calling out for help. The door was immediately opened by a Mexican girl, no more than a child herself.

"I've got a hurt woman here who needs some attention," he explained as he barged on into the room looking for a place to lay his burden down. An older Mexican woman entered, and motioned him to bring her into a back room.

He left her in care of the woman and went back into the front room. A young girl set a plate of delicious looking food on the table for him. "Gracias," he responded and sat down to eat the hot meal

Sounds of hooves beating the ground and noises of a stage pulling up outside, disturbed the quiet of the night. Keeping a grip on his plate, he moved back into the shadows of a corner of the large room.

The door swung open, and a burly, redheaded man came in, carrying what looked like mail bags. "Good evening!" he bellowed, "No passengers today? Guess everybody's getting scared to travel these roads nowadays!"

"How's that?" came a question from the shadows of a corner.

"What?" asked the burly man while squinting into the corner to see who spoke.

"Why are people afraid to travel these roads? The army escorts most of them, don't they?" came the reply.

"Well, supposed to, I reckon," was the softer answer as the big man put the bags on the table. "Just not enough of 'em anymore! During the war, most were called back east to fight, left just a handful out here in the West. Now most of the new forts being built are in Arizona where the Apaches are stirring up the most problems. Places like this one are just going to be stage stops. But these folks always have the best grub around!" He sat down and dove into the plate of food that had been placed on the table for him.

An elderly man had made a few appearances in and out of the room all evening. He was now opening the door to another group of people who had come seeking refuge at Fort Quitman. Three uniformed soldiers and two other men introduced themselves and explained they were escorting a wagon train to Fort Bliss and would be camping in the area for the evening.

The red, burly man spoke to Captain Cummings, who was now out of uniform and in regular western attire. "Howdy, where you folks hail from?"

"Just passin' through," was the curt answer from Captain Cummings.

Scout Miller, looking up from his plate, simply nodded at Tad and the soldiers. "Well," one of them exclaimed, "we wondered what happened to you!"

No questions were asked. That would have been out of line. But glances were exchanged around the room.

"How many miles on to Fort Bliss? About 70?" inquired Major Dunson. Without giving anyone time to answer, "Are there any shortcuts?" he demanded.

"No," the Mexican man who was obviously head of the house answered softly. "This is the most traveled road around. And a good road for wagons in most places. The banks of the Rio Grande seem to be trying to change its mind every other day, but for the most part it's a good road."

"I've got some injured people that could use a good night's rest. Can we use some of the old barracks here for the night?" asked the Major.

"Everything's in bad shape around here, but if it don't rain you will probably be pretty comfortable," was the answer.

The major helped the doctor bed all of the patients down, and then went into the station to have some of that good food he had seen earlier.

The wagons were all brought up, and suppers cooked, and after tending to the injured men, they passed a rather pleasant evening visiting. They discovered the stage driver's name was Jake Billingsly.

Scout Miller again entertained everyone with stories about Texas and the Southwest. He told them tales of his adventures ranging all the way from the Adobe Walls in the Panhandle to the mission at San Diego. They laughed at some of his stories and were gripped with fear at others.

Doc Turner's services were once again needed, and he took Emma with him to check on the woman that Scout Miller had brought in with him. He determined she had a slight concussion, but would be fine.

Scout Miller, who had gone with them, explained as briefly as possible how he had found her. While he was speaking, the woman suddenly announced she would like to go on with Scout Miller to Fort Bliss. Taken completely off guard, he turned red to the top of his ears!

"Well, the soldiers at the fort could probably help return you to your village," he mumbled, nervously, while turning his hat around in his hands. "I guess if you feel up to riding…"

"I will be ready," was her soft answer.

Scout left the room muttering to him self, "Yep! That's a Lady!"

About noon the next day, they all headed out toward Fort Bliss at El Paso. Captain Cummings turned and looked over his shoulder at what looked like a plume of dust hanging in the air.

"Expecting trouble?" asked a nonchalant Scout Miller.

"Always," was the answer, with a half grin.

CHAPTER SEVEN

The next water was going to be 35 miles away at a place called Birchville. Making 17 miles a day, it would be a grueling two day's journey. Luckily, the Rio Grande was always to their left, but very shallow in most places.

The men had been on edge all day. They knew someone was behind them, and one scout had not caught up with them since leaving the group to look for the captured girl. That had been almost two weeks before.

Just as they were making camp for the evening the first night after leaving Fort Quitman, they heard several horses galloping in their direction. This road appeared to be well used, but it was a time when trusting a stranger was foolish.

Matt was the first to recognize the beautiful horses of Jose Tafoya. He held his hand up to give a signal to the other men who had stepped behind rocks and other cover to hold their fire.

Then he spotted the little missing girl sitting in front of the Comanchero. He and his two companions came up to the camp as they had done previously calling out, "Hello to camp! This is your old friend, Jose!"

The little girl's mother cried out "Jenny! My little Jenny!" and ran to grab the little girl off the horse. Major Dunson reached out and held the woman back for a moment until they could make sense of what was happening.

Jose Tafoya gently lifted the child off his horse and placed her down on the ground where she went running off to the open arms of her mother. There was hardly a dry eye in camp at the sight of the child being delivered back safely.

"Thank you, oh, thank you, so much!" the mother repeated several times, looking into the eyes of the deliverer. "You are most welcome, Senora," Tafoya replied softly, with a slight bow from the waist.

The two other men had dismounted by now, also, and for the first time everyone saw that the missing scout had been riding double behind one of them. His arm was bandaged, but the man was so weak he almost fell when he attempted to walk. Major Dunson and his men immediately went to him.

Doc Turner was already grabbing his bag when they called out for him. The injured scout began telling his story while his arm was being stitched and bandaged.

"I had taken the route to the south while the other two scouts had gone west and north. I immediately picked up the trail of a carreta (a wooden wheeled wagon) with several outrider tracks. I didn't feel it was too unusual, since that is the way most of the Mexicans from

Mexico travel over that road, and I knew I was on the old Comanche Trail. It was nearing sundown on the third day out when I picked up the sound of rifle shots to the southeast. I took off in that direction. When the shots grew nearer, I staked out my horse and crawled up a small bluff to have a peek over it, not having any idea what I would find!

"About two hundred yards to my left was an Indian camp where men were hunkered down firing into some trees about fifty yards to my right. Not knowing who was who, I had about decided this wasn't my fight and started to slip away when a hand clasped over my right shoulder. It was one of the riders who had been in camp with old Tafoya! He motioned for me to follow him. We crawled through the brush for a few feet and then dropped down into an arroyo and walked into their camp as pretty as you please. They even had a campfire going and a pot of coffee ready. There were about twenty of them. I had only seen about eight men in the Indian camp and realized Tafoya's men were just taking turns shooting!

"The old man was laughing at my curious expression as he walked over and handed me a cup of coffee. In his broken English he explained that the men they were firing at had stolen some buffalo hides from them. They were planning to keep them pinned down until they ran out of supplies, which should be soon. When I told him what my mission was, his expression changed from jovial to black anger!

"He asked if this was the wagon train Scout Miller was with. I told him it was, and he motioned with two fingers toward the Indian camp. They were some of the best soldiers I had ever seen! They started advancing toward the camp, firing as they went. When they arrived at the camp, they merely stepped over the bodies of the thieves and retrieved the stolen hides.

"For the next several days I became one of them, going from one Comanchero camp to another, literally spying to see if any young girls were with them, and if they were headed to Old Mexico. He gave me strict orders to be absolutely quiet and speak to no one when we were in those camps.

"When we were in about the fifth or sixth camp I spotted the child. She was being forced to work serving food from a large kettle in the center of camp. Old Tafoya never missed a trick. He saw my head nod toward her. He gingerly went over and picked up a plate and stood in line to be served. Only about four of his men, including me, had made an appearance in the camp, so, when the other fifteen or so came thundering in, they were taken completely by surprise.

"One was leading his horse, and with one swift move he grabbed the girl, mounted his horse, and galloped away with all of the others in a cloud of dust! Of all the shouting and shooting! Man, you never heard the like!

"I didn't realize I had been wounded until we were miles away. It has taken us a few days to catch up with you, and that's the story."

Everyone was spellbound listening to the young man's story, and turned to look at Jose Tafoya. Still standing by the fire with a cup of hot coffee in his hand, he mocked a slight salute.

"I did this favor for your wagon train," he began to explain, "so that the Texas Ranger you call "Scout" Miller might give me some peace and quit chasing me all over Texas!"

"What makes you think this favor will even the score?" a voice from behind the visitors asked. Jose visibly jumped slightly, not realizing anyone had been behind him.

As he turned to face the speaker, he casually switched the coffee from his left hand to his right. A slight grin came on Scout Miller's face, along with a quick twinkle in his eyes.

"As a courtesy from one professional to another," gestured Jose with open arms. A soft laughter came from Scout Miller that surprised everyone, for they had never heard him laugh at anything!

"Are you saying that you're changing your ways, you ole' horse thief?" teased Miller back. Jose put on a face like his feelings were hurt, then burst out with laughter!

While the two of them went on bantering with fake insults, the rest of the camp went over to hug the little girl who had been returned, and to congratulate the parents.

At length Jose Tafoya and his riders parted from camp in a cloud of dust with hoots and hollers.

Scout Miller went to his saddle bags to retrieve his plate, and as casually as ever went to where Selena was dishing out a stew. He quietly began to eat his supper.

Tad, Matt, and Jasper could only look at each other in wonder at this quiet, strange man they had come to admire so much. They all now knew a little bit more about the mysterious man that they had come to care about and depend on.

The next morning they continued on their journey to the west. Everyone's water barrels were running dangerously low when the group finally arrived at a small water hole named Birchville, after James Birch, one of the original operators of the first mail service.

There were terrible stories of men not counting on the lack of water for miles in this desolate country and finally reaching the Rio Grande, only to have their thirsty horses drink so much that their sides literally split.

Jasper, Selena and the rest of the group had made friends with the other travelers. In such desolate surroundings it seemed that a woman was always starved for another woman's companionship. One of them gave Selena a beautiful hand mirror in return for her help in learning to bake bread in a Dutch oven. Selena tried to refuse the gift, but the lady insisted. It became one of Selena's prized possessions.

They all came to love Consuela, the Spanish woman that Miller had promised to take to Fort Bliss. She taught them a lot about the desert in the short time she was with them. She took Selena and Emma on walks, always with an armed escort, and showed them how the ancient Indians had survived in such a harsh environment for centuries.

Consuela also had a vast knowledge of the watering holes and springs for miles around, and in the evenings she would help the military and Scout Miller improve upon their maps.

The desert sun and wind was ever present, and the women began to feel the effects on their skin. They shared whatever they had in the way of comforts. The road had become easier to travel in most places, so everyone got out and walked some every day.

Scout Miller had been telling the group about the pretty villages that they were about to pass through, and their ages-old Spanish missions.

The area they were in used to be under Mexican rule, but since Texas joined the Union in 1845 it became part of Texas. But even before that time, a flood in 1829 put these villages on the Texas side of the Rio Grande.

The first village they came to was named San Elizario. Mostly Spanish was spoken here, and they proudly displayed 1598 as being the year their town was founded by Juan de Onate, the Spanish explorer. A post office was the most prominent building outside of the beautiful old chapel.

In 1789, when Spain still ruled Mexico, the military built a garrison to help protect the settlers in the area from the Apaches. A chapel was built inside this presidio to serve the military and their families. When Mexico won its independence from Spain, the settlers of the area continued to use this chapel.

Inside San Elizario Mission

San Elizario even boasted of a grist mill, and the travelers could buy sacks of fresh milled corn and wheat. Salt, a welcomed commodity, was mined nearby.

At noon they all enjoyed the sounds of the church bells ringing and they were invited to a celebration that evening of roasted duck and fish. They soon realized that the Mexicans didn't necessarily need a reason to celebrate; they just loved to dance and have fiestas! They called their dances a *"bailes."*

Old history abounded in this area toward El Paso, and the local Mexicans loved to tell such stories. They told of old friars who helped settle this area, of the early explorers who came from Spain, and of the descendents of these early settlers still living in the area.

Only six more miles down the road brought them to the village of Socorro. This was settled many years ago by Spanish farmers. Some of the earlier settlers had established an irrigation system that was still being used.

Socorro Mission

Destiny Road

The travelers found the mission buildings a true place of comfort and enjoyed the quiet solitude found inside. Unfortunately, floods from the Rio Grande destroyed two earlier buildings. There was a plaque dedicating this one in 1843. The walls were five feet thick, and had 26 foot-high ceilings.

The women could not help but marvel at how happy and healthy these people seemed to be in such a desolate, barren land. When asked about it, one ancient looking old man waved his arm gracefully toward the barren land and said, "Food is everywhere in the desert – if you know how to find it!"

Then he stooped down with a small kitchen knife in his hand and dug into the earth about six inches. A small root was unearthed. "Taste that," he said, as he handed it to Selena.

She wiped away as much soil as she could, and gingerly nibbled at the root. Her eyes widened in surprise, and she announced, "It tastes a lot like our sweet potato!"

He spent several minutes with them telling them about more plants of the desert that give food, and what small animals are edible. Sunflower seeds were even ground into flour, and cakes were made from it.

Ysleta Mission

Ysleta Mission Bell

Three more short miles brought them to the last of the old Spanish villages. This one was called Ysleta, another beautiful stark-white adobe church with bells announcing noon, weddings and funerals.

Another 10 miles down the road brought them to El Paso, also known as Franklin. Col. James H. Carleton was the commander of Fort Bliss. When the troops and weary travelers plodded in, they discovered that the Mexican president Benito Juarez was living there under protection of the fort. They were having their own war south of the border with the French.

Scout Miller left his ward at the fort's hospital. She was making plans to join a group that was traveling to her hometown in Sonora when he turned to leave.

"If you ever come down to my village, you will always be welcomed," she reminded him.

He said he would try, and that he hoped she got home real soon. As he walked back out to his horse, he wanted to kick himself for being such a fool. But what in the world would he do with a wife? At the moment he could think of about a hundred things.

CHAPTER EIGHT

The wagon train took two days to restock water and some of the supplies. They had already heard that once they left El Paso water would become a critical issue. One stretch of their journey alone was going to be over 60 miles between water holes.

The troop they had been traveling with had left and gone back to Fort Clark after getting supplies and picking up the new Colonel who had come in from Fort Bowie over in Arizona.

There was another escort going west heading for Cooke's Spring, also known as Fort Cummings. There again were 18 soldiers, three wagons, and two carreta's to protect this time.

As soon as they left Fort Bliss, they were entering New Mexico Territory. Fort Fillmore was the next fort on the route. Trudging over sand hills and endless miles of chaparral, the group arrived two days later at the garrison.

They could see the Organ Mountains in the distance as the New Mexico sun beat down on them. Before and during the War Between the States, the fort had developed somewhat of a shaky reputation. Claims were made that the fort's command had been left in the hands of one of the officer's wives, a Mrs. Lydia Spencer Lane, while the entire garrison, except for a sergeant and ten men, were ordered on a patrol. It also had the distinction of being the first Federal Fort to surrender completely, and without firing a shot, during the Civil War.

Some of the early commanders complained to departmental headquarters that the fort was very badly situated for defense. The truth was it had not been built for a siege, but was intended as a resting place for soldiers between Indian campaigns.

Upon arrival, they discovered this fort had also been abandoned and operations had been moved to Mesilla, about 16 miles away to the west. Already the adobe bricks were disappearing as locals were using them for their own homes.

They walked around the dust-filled parade ground and could not imagine a more forlorn place to call home.

Selena and Emma tried to be cheerful on this part of the journey, realizing that it was difficult at best for everyone. But Emma was exceptionally happy when their wagon was rolling away from such a desolate place. She could not even imagine what the army wives must have thought when brought out here from the east and being expected to make this their home.

The next day they reached the historically rich town of Mesilla. This was where the Gadsden Purchase with Mexico had been signed back in 1853. It became an important crossroads for several trade and mail routes in the following years.

Mesilla was a bustling town that could only be reached by barge because the Rio Grande River had changed its course a couple of years earlier. The downtown plaza was a busy, noisy place, filled with the sounds of animals and human laughter. The soldiers had no trouble finding the cantinas.

The saloons (or cantinas) and also barbershops were excellent places to find out the current news. Captain Cummings, Doc Turner, and Scout Miller spent about an hour at one of the cantinas the first afternoon they arrived. What they found out, they pretty well already knew. The desert was ahead of them. Water and food would be very scarce, but there were plenty of Indians.

In the troop of the 18-soldier escort, one of them was a doctor. He and Doc Turner had become fast friends. He had not seen any of the fighting in the east, but had been stationed out on the frontier during the entire war.

Captain Nathan Morse was in charge of the men. He was a seasoned Indian fighter, having been out on the desert for the last 13 years. Although small of stature, not one man under him would disobey or challenge him. He seldom smiled, and his face was so weathered it reminded people of a road map. He and Scout Miller were cut from the same pattern. He knew his business, he knew Apaches, and he also knew that if everyone wanted to survive they would have to listen to him.

He made no pretensions that he was not happy about women being along. This was extremely hard and dangerous territory, and women only made his job more difficult.

It was 60 miles from Mesilla to Cooke's Spring. They came to watering spots with such names as Picacho, Rough and Ready, and a ranch called simply Slocum's.

The Apaches had been on the warpath for a couple of years. Many wagon trains, military-supply wagons, and freighters had been ambushed in Cooke's Canyon. The road into the fort was littered with graves. Attacks on miners, travelers, herders, and military had been so numerous that the canyon had earned the name Bloody Cooke's Canyon. It was only 15 miles long, but said to be the most dangerous place in the Southwest to travel. Military records show that over 400 people were attacked and killed in about a 30- year period in Cooke's Canyon.

Everyone was watchful and alert for the entire three days it took to cross the distance. Jasper, Matt, and Tad made sure all the guns were loaded at all times. No fires were allowed the entire trip, which made life even more uncomfortable. This was the middle of the summer. The days were scorching and the nights freezing.

Cooke's Spring House Marker

Captain Morse preferred to move during the night. Apaches didn't like to fight at night, but that didn't mean they weren't prowling around. He advised that all bread and meat be cooked before ever leaving Mesilla. This was difficult, but could be done. Jasper and Selena were glad they had jerked some antelope meat along the way.

When they made reference to a "cold" camp, Emma could readily see where it got its name. The women were never to be left alone, or allowed to wander off on their own. They had heard enough stories around camp and while traveling that neither of them particularly even wanted to get out of the wagon! Doc Turner was especially attentive to the women during this branch of the journey. He and Emma were growing very fond of each other, even if both of them were denying it.

Jasper and Selena were aware of the friendship growing, but were at a loss as to how to prevent it. They had always been her slaves and servants, not her parents or advisors. Captain Cummings reminded Matt that she was only 16 years old. Matt, being nearly 10 years her senior, realized that this was certainly no place for a romance. But at the same time, he knew he was falling in love.

Emma had begun to keep a journal of their travels, and Matt would dearly love to get his hands on that little book. Selena decided not to say anything to Miss Emma unless she confided in her. After all, sixteen was not considered too young to marry.

The sun beat down on them during the day, and the miles rolled on and on during the night. The desert plants were thorny and would tear their clothes if they got too close. Several times they met freighters and even long wagon trains that were going east.

At a little past midnight, under a waning half-moon, they crossed an arroyo and headed for the dark mouth of Cooke's Canyon, about a half-mile away.

Nearing it they met the second eastbound stagecoach they had seen that night.

Stage Station at Fort Cummings

Fort Cummings had been established only two years before by Captain Valentine Dresser, Company B, and 1st Infantry of California Volunteers. The spring, which furnished a never-ending supply of fresh water for the garrison, was also the main source of friction with the Apaches.

The Apaches had used the spring as a major water source on a regular basis for many, many years. Also, Cooke's range, where Fort Cummings was built, was a route used by the Apaches since before any of the living could remember.

Ruins of Fort Cummings

When the white man first started using the area for travel, the Apaches were not alarmed. They grew more suspicious when miners started arriving in the Pinos Altos area. Then they eventually became outraged when one of their chiefs was cruelly mistreated by the miners. Many travelers paid with their lives for many years because of that atrocity.

Fort Cummings was still under construction when the group arrived that August evening. The post, situated near the famous spring, was being constructed of adobe and wood. When complete, it would be a walled fort with 10-foot high adobe walls.

Inside were officer quarters, a guardhouse, a hospital, and some storehouses. There were also corrals for the livestock.

In the morning light they could see the soldiers were busy at their different chores. Some were cutting wood that had been hauled in from the nearby wooded area, and others were making more adobe bricks, while the blacksmith clanged out a steady rhythm.

Emma was excited to be there. Her nerves had been on edge for the last three days. This seemed like a very secure place, and she wasn't too sure she ever wanted to leave!

They did plan to stay for a few days, and she was happy once again to have hot meals. She and Selena washed clothes, bought some fresh produce the locals had brought in, and baked some bread. The men were busy filling the water barrels, which had completely run dry, and visiting the sutler's store for supplies.

Doc Turner spotted some yellow ribbon and decided to give Emma some for her hair. "You know what that means in the Cavalry, don't you?" asked Tad teasingly. The Doc just grinned and made his purchase.

Jasper was standing just watching the men. Captain Cummings motioned to Jasper that there was some red ribbon that Selena might like to have. Jasper lowered his eyes. Matt Turner knew that slaves were never allowed to handle money, so Jasper had never had any money of his own to buy things with. They had used three of the $50 gold pieces, so far, and had some change left over.

Matt dug in his pocket and gave Jasper about $5 in coins. "Here, you might find something you need, just like we have." Jasper stood frozen to the ground for a long time. He had watched Doc Turner spend just a few coins on the ribbon for Miss Emma. He also knew he needed more shells for the shotgun. The sutler filled his order and gave him some change back.

Jasper had made his first purchase as a free man! He automatically handed the left over coins back to Doc Turner. But Matt just shook his head. "You're part of this trip just like we are. In fact more so!

You were asked by Emma's grandfather to bring her out here. We've still got a long way to go, so you hang on to that," and just turned and walked off.

That night Jasper couldn't wait to tell Selena about his purchases and that he actually had money in his pocket. They very carefully wrapped the left over coins in a handkerchief that Selena carried.

Matt shared with Emma the story about Jasper's first purchase as he was giving her the ribbon. Tears rolled down Emma's cheeks as she sat watching how excited Jasper and Selena were. "No, Grandfather wouldn't ever let them have money of their own. It just wasn't done. I always thought it odd that keys to everything on the place were entrusted to Jasper, but not any money! It's going to be a different world from now on," she said softly.

"By the way," Matt said, "do you know that when a soldier in the cavalry gives a girl a yellow ribbon and she wears it, it means that she's his girl?"

"Well! I wouldn't want to be misunderstood then," she replied while tying the ribbon around her thick braid. Matt couldn't resist bending down and kissing her on the nose.

Emma thought her heart would beat out of her chest. What a time and place to fall in love!

They were still in some of the most dangerous country in the Southwest, and the next stop was almost another 18 miles. They were again assigned to another group of soldiers headed toward Fort Bowie. These were all seasoned cavalry soldiers that looked just like Captain Morse and Scout Miller.

They discovered quickly that the same rules applied as before. There would be no fires and no wandering off. These men were of the same mind when it came to women being out here, so Selena and Emma tried their best to stay out of their way.

Scout Miller told them more stories of how the Apaches were famous for disguising themselves to look like the terrain. And the group still had to go through Cooke's Canyon, which was the part of the trip most dreaded by all.

They all listened attentively to a story about his having known an Apache guide who at one time had shown him how Apaches can camouflage themselves to look like rocks, trees, or even the ground. Ever since that demonstration, he never trusted his eyes to simply scan the terrain. Anything out of the ordinary made him study it thoroughly.

He was thinking on all of this the next morning while they leaving Fort Cummings. Suddenly, he realized that a rock off to the side of him didn't look quite right. The hair on his neck stood up! The shadows were all wrong, and for that matter, the tumbleweed that was near it didn't look like it belonged either. Maybe he was just seeing things, but those intuitions had kept him alive this long.

Suddenly a moccasin appeared at the corner of the rock. Scout Miller didn't even remember aiming his rifle. He quickly fired into the tumbleweed, and a scream followed the report of the second rifle shot.

They had just entered the canyon past the spring. This was one of the Apaches favorite ambush places.

The ground suddenly seemed to stand up in front of him! The Apaches had literally buried themselves in the sand as a disguise!

The soldiers were already firing and all the horses were running full speed. Scout Miller nearly ran down an Indian that had suddenly stood up directly in front of him! He jerked his horse to the left and looked back over his shoulder and there was nothing there! Just as quickly, he was gone.

He caught a glimpse of a grey rock that looked just like the one earlier, so he fired into it. This time the bullet ricocheted and shale splattered! It was a real one.

Jasper was driving the wagon and firing one of the pistols at the same time. He was becoming a real Westerner.

The women were in the back of the wagon trying their best to load the guns that were kept there while at the same time holding on to keep from getting thrown around.

The Indians weren't expecting 20 outriders along with the wagons! They decided to come back another day. By everyone's count, they must have lost at least 10 of their tribe that day. Only one of the soldiers had been hit, and it was a minor wound.

As the cavalry doctor tended to the soldier, Doc Turner went back to check on their group. Except for a few scratches and bruises, everyone was fine.

No one was inclined to spend much time in the canyon as sitting targets, so they got underway as quickly as possible.

Destiny Road

They had to pass through a couple of more ambush sites that the Apaches liked to use before being out of immediate danger, but Miller was fairly sure the Indians had had enough for one day.

At around 4:00 P.M. they stopped for the day to rest and eat. They would be pulling out again around 3:00 A.M.

The distance from Fort Cummings to Fort Bowie was about 120 miles. If they averaged 12 miles a day, it would take them almost two weeks to get there, barring no bad weather, no more Indian attacks, or any of the other hundreds of mishaps that can befall travelers in such dangerous country.

They were able to find three more good water holes before arriving at Fort Bowie. The names the soldiers called these places were all in Spanish, such as, *Ojo del la Vaca,* and P*eloncillo.*

Emma loved to sit in the cool of the evenings and wonder about the people who had settled such a harsh land so many years ago. The Spanish had apparently been here already for centuries, but people of Indian tribes were living here in this barren land long before them! Where had they come from? How did they master this environment?

The sunsets in the evenings looked like a painting from one of the 'Old Master Painters' and never failed to leave the travelers spellbound.

Scout Miller told them of explorers and trail blazers who had come through this land in years past. Most of them had been on military expeditions that were also surveying possible roads and railroad routes.

One of the water holes they depended turned out to be completely dry. One day without water in this country, and a traveler and his animals could be in serious trouble.

Everyone was on the alert. Many stories of surprise attacks were remembered by the military escort as some of the men killed had been comrades of theirs.

Cemetery at Fort Bowie

They passed by the Apache Springs which was another source of contention with the Apaches. They also rolled as quietly as possible by an old stage station and the post cemetery.

Every able-bodied person in the wagon train that had a rifle or gun had his weapon loaded and easily accessible. Most of the women were taught, as had Emma and Selena, to load and shoot.

When they arrived at Fort Bowie they found another busy fort which had been established only a few years back. Their first sight of the fort found it enveloped by a smoky haze. Building was going on, and everyone seemed to have his own job to do. Bricks were being made, logs were being cut, and a garden was being planted. Again they felt a strong sense of relief regarding their safety.

The fort lay at the foot of Dos Cabezas Mountains, and to the south were the Chiricahua Mountains, home of the Chiricahua Apaches. Every soldier and traveler of that era knew that Fort Bowie lay at the foot of those mountains.

Ruins of Fort Bowie

Emma and Matt had noticed on arriving near the foot of the mountains two hills on top that really did look like two heads peeking over the top of the mountain. Scout Miller had told them that *Dos Cabezas* meant 'two heads' in Spanish. They found themselves truly falling in love with the west, in spite of all of the immediate dangers.

There was talk of moving the fort to a better location several hundred feet to the south of this temporary fort, so they assumed many of the new bricks would be used for the new buildings.

Again they lost their escort as Fort Bowie was their destination. They were told they would have to wait nearly a week for an escort to take them on to Tucson. The commander of the fort was not willing for them to leave on their own, and insisted that they wait.

The women found some officers' wives who had just arrived, and they enjoyed each other's company immensely. Selena was always trying to wait on them, which made Emma very uncomfortable even though most of the ladies accepted it.

The days passed quickly, and the escort was ready to leave earlier than promised. This time the cavalry had a huge wagon to haul along with them in which to bring back supplies. The going would be slower than they had anticipated.

These were also seasoned troopers, but they traveled altogether differently from the other officers. They were on the road by five o'clock every morning, stopping for the day at around three o'clock in the afternoon. Fires were welcomed every evening.

Scout Miller had been over this trail to California twice and had been over the Oregon Trail once. On the previous evening he unrolled a map that was drawn on leather that included this particular area.

Captain Nichols was very interested in comparing their military map with Miller's, as the army's was several years old. He noticed that Fort Bowie was on his map, but not Fort Cummings.

The Butterfield Mail Route, the Beale Expedition Road, and several others were drawn on Miller's, but all that the Army map had was the trail of Gen. Kearny, the Santa Fe Trail, and little else.

Destiny Road

The captain was very impressed to find several passes and stage station stops which were marked on Miller's that he did not have on his own. He worked copying, and revising his map into the wee hours of the morning. He knew how valuable a true lay of the land was out here in the Southwest.

The roads through the pass leaving Apache Springs became so narrow and rough that Scout Miller suggested everyone who could walk do so. In some areas men had to stand on the wheels to keep the wagons from turning over. All of this was done while a detachment of soldiers and scouts guarded both ends of the wagon train. It took them several hours to go only a few miles.

On the second day out they camped on a beautiful clear stream called the San Pedro. Numerous old adobe ruins along the banks were a reminder that this country has been lived in by humans for many years.

Wildlife was abundant, as were varieties of cactus. Many of the travelers were in need of fresh meat, but they were discouraged from firing their rifles for fear that Apaches might be near. The seasoned soldiers showed them how to set traps, and snares, for small animals, and thus save on ammunition.

On the fifth day out from Fort Bowie, they arrived at the beautiful mission of San Xavier.

This stark white church was lovingly known as the White Dove of the Desert. As the white billowy clouds drifted by against the surreal blue sky, the sight was absolutely breathtaking.

San Xavier Mission

The priest there told them they had been trying to start a school there for some time for the Indian children, but that the children's parents refused to allow them to attend.

Several of the weary travelers found the cool, quiet sanctuary of the mission chapel very refreshing. Most of them were not Catholic but had missed the peacefulness churches can bring.

From there they went north eight miles to Tucson. All of the inhabitants were Mexican except for a few military men and travelers. All of the houses and buildings were made of adobe. The town was quite lively, and again they were treated to the fast-paced music which was commonly heard in this area.

The detachment of soldiers that was leading moved them through town rather quickly, and they set up camp outside of town by a cool refreshing stream.

CHAPTER NINE

Tucson was an old Mexican town busy with trading and several cantinas. It had become a leading town in Arizona, largely absent of any kind of civil law. Consequently, every man had become a law unto himself. Private quarrels were the unfortunate explanation for the population growth in the graveyards.

The town had long been remembered by its inhabitants as an old military post. Many years ago the Spanish troops had been stationed there, and had been paid in silver coin. Money had been plentiful then, and goods from Sonora had been brought up on pack animals. Then in 1849 the Mexican government took a step that would forever sever any chance of peace between Mexico and the Apaches: Chihuahua reinstituted the bounty for Indians, offering 250 pesos for each live warrior, 200 for adult male scalps, and 150 pesos for each female or child taken captive.

Armed with spears, clubs, and bows and arrows, the Apache became more angry and murderous than ever before.

After the Gadsden Purchase ratifications were made in 1854, Tucson fell under the jurisdiction of the United States, and officially become a territory in 1863.

Many U.S. soldiers were in town, their detachments going to several points around, two of them being Fort Goodwin and Fort Bowie.

Again Tad and Matt decided to spend a couple of hours visiting the cantinas for local news. Everyone was talking about some travelers from Texas who had been attacked and killed by the Indians. It had happened somewhere north of where they had just passed.

A cold shiver ran down Tad's spine as he remembered that on more than one occasion on this trip they had been a little early or just a little late, or just a little to the north or south of some terrible happenings. He truly felt they must have an angel from Heaven watching over them.

It was a common consensus that anyone traveling these days should do so only with a military escort. Only the foolhardy would attempt to go it alone.

The captain who was in charge of the group handed them over to a regiment going all the way to Fort Yuma, an almost 300 mile trip. There were three other wagons assigned to the escort, and the announcement was made for everyone to be ready to leave in two days.

One of the families that had joined the group were the O'Sullivan's. The man was called "Sully". The mother of the family was Margaret. The contrast in personalities between the two couldn't have been greater.

Sully was a hard and bitter man, who spoke harshly to everyone, and in general wasn't well liked or respected. Margaret, on the other hand always had a quick smile and pleasing personality.

The two children in this family were Tully, who appeared to be about sixteen years old, and his younger sister Sally. Both of the children looked considerably like their mother, and fortunately, had her pleasing disposition.

Selena and Emma were again busy washing clothes and baking bread. They had been told there were no forts between here and Fort Yuma, but there were small communities. Some supplies could be bought, but everyone was encouraged to stock up in Tucson.

One evening Selena baked biscuits in her Dutch oven and decided to share with the new family. Margaret and the children were expressing delight over the gift of food that was brought over in a cloth napkin, when the father suddenly appeared.

Mr. O'Sullivan grabbed the napkin out of his wife's hands and shoving it back rudely to Selena, said "Go feed yer own kind!"

Tad and Matt immediately had to restrain Jasper, who was watching the scene only a few feet away.

Over the span of the next few weeks, Sully O'Sullivan's outbursts of temper made life miserable for anyone around him, but especially his own family.

It was not generally accepted for anyone to interfere in another's business, but his actions were hard to ignore.

Before leaving Tucson Tad, Matt, and Jasper went to the general store with a list from Selena for flour, salt, sides of bacon, beans, coffee, and vinegar. Tad also remembered to pick up more matches, which he stored in a tightly-corked bottle, to protect against moisture and mice. One hundred pounds of bacon came packed in a box which was surrounded by bran to help keep the fat from melting away. The sugar was packed in rubber sacks to keep out moisture. The flour also was in one-hundred-pound sacks, only these were made of canvas. The dried beans and the coffee beans came in burlap sacks weighing twenty pounds each. The vinegar came in gallon jugs. Selena used vinegar for cooking and cleaning, so the men decided that two gallons was best.

When the day of departure arrived, they were ready to pull out at five o'clock in the morning along with everyone else. The soldiers had camped about a mile from town, but were ready and in line when the order was given. The wagons were placed near the back of the line with a detachment of soldiers behind.

Col. Pollack was in charge of the regiment. As was with most seasoned military men, he was pretty much a no nonsense type. He was continually sending out scouting parties, sometimes as many as four in all directions. Usually there were five to twelve men in each party.

Scout Miller went with several different parties and was gone for days at a time. All they ever reported was seeing Indian signs, but were never involved in any skirmishes.

Since it was the middle of the summer, the heat was almost unbearable. All of the women and children wore bonnets to keep as much sun off of them as possible.

It was becoming more apparent that Selena was with child. As it was not proper to talk about such things, Emma began to do more and more of the camp chores to allow Selena an occasional well-deserved rest.

Tucson Desert Area

With the sparse desert everywhere about them, they all began to enjoy seeing a small forest of tall tree- like cacti they learned to identify as Saguaros. Some rose to a height of at least forty feet. The Indians had a belief that these were their ancestors who had come back to protect them.

While sitting together in the evenings and viewing these majestic cacti, Matt and Emma could see how someone's imagination could run away with him and he might begin seeing human forms in these plants.

Wood began to be scarce, and water was used only when necessary for cooking. Whenever they came upon water barrels and canteens were filled first. Washing and bathing were always done in the evening. Everyone bathed clothed, mainly because it was dangerous country, and also because soldiers were picketed everywhere. Privacy was non-existent.

At the first camp outside Tucson they found a good well. Antelope had been brought in by some of the scouts and the fresh meat was welcomed.

Much visiting went on between the travelers of the wagons, and meals were nearly always shared. It was understood by all however, not to mingle with the soldiers. Each had their own duty to do every day, and most took their jobs seriously. They knew that their and the travelers' lives literally depended on their competence.

All continued to witness Sully O'Sullivan's abuse to his children and wife. His son had suffered severe bruises from being beat with a large stick, the wife had had a plate of food thrown at her, and the daughter was slapped very hard one morning over some indiscretion known only to them. It was becoming harder and harder for the other men to tolerate such behavior.

Other than that, and the heat, the trip was going well for most. They were learning how to cope in the desert.

Emma liked to watch the scouts look out over the terrain. Many of them used tobacco, and they would sit on their horses, slowly chewing, and hardly moving their heads for long periods of time. She knew their eyes were always moving and watching the shadows of bushes and rocks. Scout Miller talked in the evenings about how the Apaches were masters at disguising themselves. She found herself becoming more aware of her surroundings.

Destiny Road

Another thing she noticed was that no soldier, nor the men in her own group, ever stared into the fires at night. She and Selena found great comfort in watching the fire burn, but none of the men would sit with them. She finally asked Matt why he wouldn't come and sit with her in the evening. He explained that looking into a fire will temporarily blind you, and in enemy territory you can't afford to be handicapped.

Emma and Selena found the company of other women very comforting. The other travelers were headed for Los Angeles and one family was going as far as San Francisco. One of the ladies would even put a tablecloth on a small table for them to have tea. Small luxuries went a long way out in the desert.

Emma befriended a little girl who was practicing her handwriting one evening. She noticed that Selena was watching very intently as she helped the child make her letters correctly.

When they were alone, she asked Selena if she would like to learn to write. "More than anything!" was the excited reply. "Then I could teach my chilluns!"

Emma began to work with Selena and Jasper every evening teaching them how to read and write. It was exciting to see how eager they were to learn each new letter.

Some of the water they came upon was brackish and unfit to drink, although the animals seemed to enjoy it. As they continued on they passed by several old stage stations, most of which had good wells.

One morning they all read an inscription on a pole that they came upon: P & M Reservation 1858. Scout Miller explained to them that it stood for Pima & Maricopa Indian Reservation.

The road was almost level in places, which helped them make better time. But now the country consisted totally of desert plants, and Emma found herself daydreaming of the cool lovely pine trees they had passed through only a few weeks back.

One evening Scout Miller amused everyone by telling them of a great canyon to the north of them. "About two hundred miles nearly directly north of us", he began, "is a canyon like nothing you've ever seen before. In places it's a mile deep and nearly 20 miles across." He seemed to end his story as he reached for the coffee pot to refill his cup.

After a period of time of staring at him incredulously, the group around him began to shift their gaze to each other to see if anyone else was buying this story. A soft chuckle emerged from the darkness, and Col. Pollack went up to the fire and also reached for the coffee pot.

"Well, it does sound rather farfetched, but it's true. It's called the Grand Canyon. Miller, you ever been there?" he asked in a soft monotone voice.

"Yep" was the brief answer, "twice." Then after a period of silence, he added: "Some of the early Spanish explorers thought they were the first men to ever see it. They hiked around it for months, even planted some fruit trees so that when they came back that way they would have some food. Then they found some old ruins of a people that had lived there long before they were there, and later they found an Indian tribe still living near one of the rims! Somebody once wrote that there's nothing new under the sun!"

Emma had to grin to herself and realize that this hard old man had probably had a sweet mother read the Bible to him in his youth!

Occasionally they would meet another wagon train or detachment of soldiers heading east. Once they came upon a group of emigrants that had not taken the necessary provisions, and appeared to be in a bad way. They gave them a few rations, and their wagons were put behind the others and escorted on into Fort Yuma.

On the Gila River they found a small tribe of Indians growing watermelons and wheat. Some of the men went fishing after camp was made, and that evening they shared a virtual banquet.

The next day they came upon a larger village of four or five thousand inhabitants. These were the Pima and Maricopa Indians. They were told that these tribes were allied against the Apaches. Apparently the hereditary hatred went deep.

A company of Indian scouts was stationed there under the command of Lieut. Walker. The other soldiers enjoyed visiting with Walker and discovered that the scouts were very effective in fighting the Apaches in their own way.

The villages were extremely neat. The houses were constructed of some sort of willow branches, and the tops were thatched with grass and dirt. They had small gardens fenced in with poles.

They discovered that one of the buildings even housed a 10-horse-power steam flour mill. While walking about the village, they came upon a blacksmith shop, and even a primitive restaurant.

They were told that the next leg of the journey would be 45 miles with no water wells or streams. No one was looking forward to this.

While sitting a little way from a camp fire, Emma realized how much she was really enjoying the desert. During the day she constantly saw new plants and enjoyed the little yellow birds that darted from tree to tree. The evenings were extremely quiet, and the stars shone so brightly you could almost count them.

Scout Miller had been telling the stories of the mountain gods that the Indians had believed in for hundreds of years. These stories had been handed down through numerous generations by song and storytelling. Emma's favorites were those of people in need being helped by these spirits. She didn't know whether or not to really believe the stories. She couldn't even decide to believe the story about the Grand Canyon yet! This was truly a mystical place.

They were hoping to arrive in Gila Bend, a town named after the river, in four days time.

CHAPTER TEN

The road was much like what they had already been traveling over, with the exception that they were seeing fewer of the Saguaros. Most of the desert plants had some kind of thorns or stickers. Occasionally an unobserving person would let out a yelp, and everyone would know that the desert had found another victim.

Thunderstorms came up suddenly, and the downpours felt good after all the heat and dust. Usually strong winds accompanied them, but these died down in the afternoons and evenings.

After one particular storm, the cover over the wagon needed repair, but Jasper was aware that they could not take the time, so it was pulled back down as tightly as possible and tied temporarily back in place.

Emma and Selena had baked bread and prepared some beans before the long trek to Gila Bend. Even with the prospects of finding no water after leaving the Indian villages, most of the travelers had prepared enough ahead of time to make the journey quite well.

Mesquite wood and cottonwood were brought in for the fires at night. A few sparse willows showed themselves here and there. Small birds and the trails of small reptiles were all the wildlife they saw, but the scouts told stories of encountering occasional mountain lions, javelinas, squirrels, and even a white tailed deer.

Scorpions and tarantulas were also abundant! Everyone began sleeping up off the ground, and making sure to shake out his boots and shoes in the mornings before sticking his toes in them!

Maricopa Wells, named after the Indians living nearby, was the first dry tank they came to. Stopping for lunch and making coffee, the soldiers refilled their canteens from the water barrels, and then journeyed on for a few more miles before making camp.

The next day they saw the last of the tall Saguaros and continued on to the remains of an old stage station that was said to be a half-way mark between Gila Bend and Maricopa Wells. True to what they had been told, there was no water.

On the fourth day without finding even a spring, they finally made it to the small community and were refreshed by the narrow river flowing through the desert.

Gila Bend was located on the Gila River. A few white people lived there, and several Mexican families. Watermelons were plentiful, and they were also selling "Tarantula Juice," a strong drink concoction that only the soldiers would try.

Two other emigrant trains were camping there, and one supply train going to Camp McDowell. Another Cavalry company of California Volunteers arrived about the same time as the wagon train rolled in.

Destiny Road

The population of the small town tripled in a matter of hours. Never needing a reason for a *fandango*, the local Mexican families invited everyone to a dance that evening. The gaiety and lively music helped improve the spirits of all.

Emma had been saving her best dress for just such an occasion. She and Matt had only danced once when a handsome lieutenant from the supply train took her away. She lost count of all the new young men that took her around the dance floor that evening.

Tad Cummings couldn't help but tease Matt that he had better lay claim to that young lady before some dashing lieutenant swept her off her feet!

Matt and Emma did get to dance together a few more times that evening, and it was midnight before they made their way back to the wagon.

Jasper was waiting up for them, and once again Matt realized that Jasper felt it his duty to get Miss Emma to her father as was promised. After escorting Emma to the wagon where she and Selena were sharing sleeping quarters, he went over and sat down beside Jasper.

"You know," he began, "I didn't plan on falling in love with Emma when we began this trip. But I do love her, and she loves me. But I also respect your promise to her grandfather. Now, I'm making a promise to you that I will help you in every way that I can. I do plan to ask for her hand in marriage, but I'll take that up at the right time with her father."

Matt had said every word while looking straight into Jasper's eyes. Jasper stood up, leaned on his rifle for a moment, and then shook hands with Matt. Without ever saying a word, he had made peace with Matt.

The travelers were getting used to the military routine: The sound of "reveille" that awoke them early every morning, followed immediately by the "roll call". Then came "general", which meant for all hands to hurry up and get ready for the road. About an hour later "assembly" would sound, and the soldiers would fall in to await the call "forward", the signal to head out.

Along the Gila River were occasional heavy willows, weeds, and a few cottonwood trees. The next evening was another stop by the Gila called Canyon Station.

The road was becoming very rough and rocky. They only made twelve miles before coming to a place named Oatman Flat. Scout Miller related a story to them of a family by the name of Oatman who had been massacred near there. Several of the children were captured, and one of the daughters lived to tell of the harrowing experience later in life.

A small burnt rock that resembled smooth lava covered the ground for miles. All were curious, but there seemed to be no explanation for it.

Oatman Family Monument

That evening all five of the group, except for Scout Miller, walked over to see a marker that others of the group had already seen and told about.

It was a burial place for the family that was murdered by the Apaches. The marker read "The Oatman Family, 1851." This only heightened the sense of fear everyone was already feeling.

Emma sat on the incline that led up to the marker, and tried to envision the terrible scene when the Indians had attacked and taken the captives. They were so close to California to have come all this way just to die.

Part of the trail they were on was the Santa Fe Trail. That probably explained why they were meeting so many freighters going back east.

The road began to smooth out again and turned into a beautiful grass plain. They decided to stop early and turn the oxen, mules, and other animals out on the grass. Again, as always, scouting parties came and went under the direction of the colonel.

The country didn't change much, and the river was never more than a mile away. On several evenings, if the colonel permitted, men from the wagon train went fishing. Jasper once again proved his outdoor abilities and brought in a big mess of fish. Selena and Emma were delighted to add something different to the table. In fact, Jasper was able to share his catch with several of the families.

The desert is a strange yet enchanting place. The days too hot, and the nights were uncomfortably cold. The smell of the grass with the sun beating down on it was very pleasant. New kinds of cactus enchanted them with every passing mile.

For several days now the scouts had been warning everyone about the dangers of rattlesnakes. They seemed to be plentiful. Occasionally one was shot and the meat put in a stewpot. Selena told Jasper, no matter how bad things got, she didn't think she could eat a snake. Everyone in the group noticed how Selena was getting large with child, but as protocol of the time would have it, nothing was mentioned out loud.

One morning, a scream from the O'Sullivan camp sent everyone running over to see what had happened this time. Expecting another atrocity from Sully O'Sullivan, they instead found him the victim of a rattlesnake bite on the leg and hand. "Doc" Matt Turner worked feverously to help save the poor man, but by noon that day, he was dead. His leg and hand had swelled up and turned completely black.

The rest of that day was spent burying him, and having a solemn reading over him. To no one's surprise, the family did very little mourning. The colonel told the wife one of his soldiers could be of service to help drive their wagon, but she kindly refused, stating that her son would now be the man of the family.

Almost as if nothing had happened, they lined up the next morning with the other wagons and proceeded on toward Fort Yuma.

Occasionally there were signs of mining that had gone on in years past, but nothing in the present. The scouts that had been in this area for years said the abandoned diggings were old copper mines.

They came to several small ranchos inhabited by Mexicans. At a nice grove called Grinnell's Station, a white man with his Mexican wife came out to greet them. The couple shared a community meal with the group, as they could not have fed everyone, and then the man entertained them with beautiful music played on a twelve-stringed guitar.

The next day they made camp at the foot of Antelope Peak. The mountain rose abruptly to several hundred feet. The only wood they could find was small pieces of mesquite. That night was almost too cool for comfort, so Emma and Selena added more blankets to their bedding.

They knew they were getting near Fort Yuma when one morning they met a detachment from the fort on its way to Fort Goodwin with supplies. While watering the teams at Swiveller's Ranch, they met another detachment heading for Fort Breckenridge.

Twenty days after leaving Tucson, they finally arrived in Fort Yuma. The Colorado River and the Gila met there. The fort was built a short distance away on the western bank of the Colorado. All the buildings were built of adobe with flat roofs.

The noise and dust were nearly unbearable as there were several military detachments camping there. They were all waiting to be assigned to frontier forts in Arizona Territory.

Fort Yuma Monument

Yuma Crossing Marker

Colorado River at Yuma Crossing

The wagon train was directed to camp on the east side of the fort and wait for further instructions. It was decided that Jasper was to stay with the wagon and team, while Tad and Matt announced that they needed to run an errand.

Emma, being very curious, started to follow Matt but was turned back with strict instructions not to leave Jasper and Selena. Matt was sure that she was pouting, and had to grin about it.

Tad Cummings and Matt Turner went quickly to the telegraph office located at the Fort. They had received a message from Richard Barker stating that he would be meeting them at Fort Yuma to pick up his daughter on or around August 30, 1865.

Unknowingly to Emma, they had sent a telegram to her father from Tucson. As briefly as possible, they explained that they were on their way west to bring Emma to him. They had sent it to San Diego, his last-known address.

They went to the local hotel, and sure enough, a Richard Barker was checked in as of yesterday. Matt and Tad went to the door of his room, and Matt knocked softly.

A nice-looking man in his early forties answered. They introduced themselves, and Richard Barker was nearly overcome by emotion. While taking him out to where the wagon was camped, they told him that his being here would be a tremendous surprise to Emma, as she knew nothing of his coming here for her.

An hour later he was holding his precious daughter to his chest as if he would never let her go. He was also telling them that he had booked passage on the steamer *Senator* to take them down the Colorado River, then around the Baja Peninsula to San Diego, instead of going across land. It was to leave in three days time.

Scout Miller came by the wagon to tell them all good-bye. Friendships made on journeys like this one are lasting ones. When asked where he was going, he said, with a twinkle in his eye, that he might go down Sonora way to see an old friend.

Richard Barker reminded Jasper and Selena that they were part of their family and he had already made plans for them in San Diego. A new beginning can be frightful, but exciting!

Matt let his plans be known that he wanted to see Emma to her new home. Her father, becoming immediately aware that there was something special between the two, invited them all to travel with them.

Three days later the huge steamer pulled out of dock and headed down the Colorado River, out into the open water of the Gulf of California, then on around to San Diego.

The manifest listed a Mr. Richard Barker and daughter, Emma; a Mr. And Mrs. Jasper Barker; Dr. Matt Turner; and a Mr. Tad Cummings - who just wanted to see how things ended.

Epilogue

The pale yellow jeep came to a halt and dust rose from its tires as two young women got out and peered over the bank of the Colorado River. They were visiting the old Fort Yuma in August, 1995.

One was tall and had beautiful smooth chocolate skin. The other was petite and blonde. They weren't really related, but sisters couldn't have been closer.

In just over a month, they would be leaving for individual colleges hundreds of miles apart. They had talked about taking this trip all of their lives and knew that now was the right time, or they might never get to do it.

As Emma Caldwell, named after her ancestor, put on her sunglasses against the glaring sun, she couldn't help but be reminded that no one going west in 1865 had ever even heard of sunglasses.

They both wished they had their great-great grandmothers to talk to and go over every inch of the country that they had traveled all those years ago. But they were on their own and armed only with a small journal that Emma Barker Turner had kept.

They would start at the end of the journal and go forward, and therefore retrace that incredible journey backwards, mainly because that's where they lived, at the journal's end in San Diego, California.

Bags were packed, and cameras were ready as they started their own journey back in time.

"How to Get There"

Most of the travels in the beginning of the story are on the Old San Antonio Road and Old Spanish Road, known to us as State Highway 21. This was a great thoroughfare of pioneer Texas, stretching 1,000 miles from Saltillo, Mexico, to present-day Louisiana. The general route followed ancient Indian and buffalo trails.

Over the centuries, explorers, traders, outlaws, military men, and civilians traversed this road. It was also known as *El Camino Real*.

The Overland Mail Route of the San Antonio-San Diego Route on the lower road is following an established route between watering places. This route was also used extensively by the military and other early travelers and traders.

Apparently this lower road had several names, some of which were the Butterfield Trail, Cooke's Wagon Road, and Gila Trail. But one name that the pioneers of the 1860s used was <u>*Destiny Road*</u>, probably because it aroused hopes of a new beginning in the hearts of the travelers.

So this is where our story begins:

Marshall, Texas – is located on I-20 approximately 39 miles west of Shreveport, Louisiana. This city played a major role during the Civil War for the Confederacy. A beautiful courthouse, museum and at least 15 homes and buildings listed in the National Register for Historic Places can be viewed and visited.

Nacogdoches – located on SH 21 is one of the oldest settlements in Texas. The town offers beautiful antebellum homes and an interesting historic downtown area.

Crockett – also located on State Highway 21 was named for David Crockett. The community served as a mustering and training point for the Confederacy during the Civil War. This town boasts of many beautiful old homes and a Fiddlers Festival each June.

Madisonville – still on SH 21, has a beautiful old brick courthouse built in 1894, and a picturesque old hotel with lots of history.

Kurten – still on SH 21, was settled by a German named Henry Kurten in the early 1850's. He carried freight between Mexico and Brazos County. New German settlers were invited to work on his farm for the passage over during the following years. Today it is a small community.

Bryan – still heading southwest on SH 21, was an early settlement named for a nephew of Stephen F. Austin. The town was a vital distribution center during the Civil War for freight and troops for the Confederacy. Settled by German, Czech and Italian immigrants in the late 1800's, many of their descendants still reside there. Bryan is home to Texas A&M University, and the oldest existing Carnegie Library in Texas is also located here.

Caldwell – continuing on is this Czech settlement founded in the 1800's. They host a wonderful *"Czech" Out Kolache* festival held in September.

Bastrop – still on SH 21, is home of one of the oldest Opera Houses. The town is chocked full of antique shops, historical homes, and beautiful pines.

San Marcos – the "Jewel of the Corridor" is home to Texas State University, and the best outlet mall shopping in the Southwest.

The earliest recorded history is that the area was explored by Alonso de Leon's men in 1689. The beautiful present courthouse was built in 1909, and the town has an interesting historic State Bank (1891). Victorian homes can be seen on tree-lined streets.

New Braunfels – approximately 30 miles east of San Antonio, this beautiful community was settled by hard working German farmers and craftsmen. More antique shops and beautiful furniture can be found here.

San Antonio – at the cross roads of I-10 & I-35, this area is one of the most historic in Texas. Early Spanish missions were established here, one being the famous *Alamo*. Historical sites at Fort Sam Houston can be visited, but keep in mind that it is still an active military installation. The "River Walk" is a beautiful place for families to visit and shop.

Castroville – Heading west out of San Antonio on US 90, this small community has been home to many peoples and nationalities. The Landmark Inn, built around 1844, by a French settler, is a good place to start for local history.

Uvalde - Also on US 90, this pretty city calls itself "The Best Kept Secret in the West!" Visitors can enjoy everything from bird watching to exploring caverns. On North Getty Street you can visit the home of John Nance Garner, who was Vice-President under Franklin D. Roosevelt. There is an interesting Pioneer Cemetery where the burial site of King Fisher (who was an outlaw turned lawman) can be seen with other interesting gravesites. Other local heroes you can read all about at a local museum located in a restored Opera House.

Fort Clark – Established 1852 had a wonderful military history that every American and history "buff" should visit. Many famous officers served at Fort Clark, and a number of streets and buildings at the fort honor their names. Near the fort off of US Highway 90 there is also a Seminole-Negro Indian Scout Cemetery, where four Medal of Honor recipients have specially marked graves. A beautiful picnic area with ancient oak and pecan trees is where the pioneers bound for California camped on the overland trail.

Camp Hudson – located on the right bank of the Devils River, some 40 miles northwest of Del Rio, Texas. In 1936 the Texas Historical Commission placed a centennial marker at the site. However, by the 1980s no buildings were standing. Site is located south of Ozona, Texas on Hwy. 163.

Fort Lancaster – Is a partially restored fort with an available tour. There is an interesting old fort cemetery with the headstones of the children's graves that are mentioned in the story. This is located 8 miles east of Sheffield off I-10 on U.S. Hwy. 290. Take exit 325 off of I-10.

Comanche Springs (Fort Stockton) – the fort was established in 1859 to protect travelers on the stage route. The original fort was burned at the end of the Civil War by Confederate Troops, but was completely rebuilt in 1867 by Federal Troops of the 9th U.S. Cavalry. The small town of Fort Stockton offers a 16 passenger tour bus that goes through the historic district. The Annie Riggs Museum is a "must-see."

Fort Davis – This is a well preserved fort that was built in 1850s -1880s containing 460 acres in breathtaking beautiful country. Local attractions include McDonald Observatory of the University of Texas, the First Rural School West of Pecos River, and an interesting old cemetery that includes the grave of an Indian girl that was killed while warning of an impending massacre. Located on Texas State Rd. 17, south of Balmorhea in Jeff Davis County.

Van Horn Wells – The wells were the only dependable water supply in this arid terrain back when the San Antonio-San Diego Mail Route passed through this area. Visitors can enjoy Red Rock Ranch, which offers scenic driving tours and guided hikes. There is also the movie set constructed for "Lonesome Dove" in the area. Van Horn, Texas is located at the intersection of U.S. Hwys. 80 & 90 and State Hwy. 54 in Culberson County.

Fort Quitman – is now on private land near the Rio Grande River, but there is not much left of it. Off of I-10, take exit 87 onto Farm Road 34. Locals may be of help to locate.

San Elizario, Socorro, and Ysleta - are communities that have now been engulfed into the city of El Paso. All still have beautiful old missions that can be visited on what is called the "Mission Trail" located on State Rd. 20.

El Paso – (Ft. Bliss) was also called Franklin in the 19th Century. This area was a scheduled stop for stages and mail routes. Established 1849, was part of the frontier defense system for the protection of travelers going to California. Present day city of nearly a million people is located on I-10 at the most western point of Texas.

Fort Fillmore – was established 1851 and closed in 1862, was also called Brazito. It claimed a Post Office from 1852-1863. The remains of the fort lie on a private pecan farm south of Las Cruces, N.M.

La Mesilla – is listed several times in archives as part of the Overland Mail Route. From Mesilla to the next scheduled stop (Cooke's Spring) was 60 miles! Mesilla, New Mexico, today is located on I-10 just southwest of Las Cruces. Historians note that this is the town where the Gadsden Purchase was signed in 1853.

Cooke's Spring – is located near Fort Cummings in Cooke's Range (see Fort Cummings below). Cooke's Spring has been important for survival since pre-historic times. The spring house can still be visited (see directions to fort ruins below).

Fort Cummings – Established 1863 for the protection of travelers, the fort seemed to deter Indian attacks for a couple of years. Cooke's Canyon, located nearby, was one of the most dangerous places to travel in the Southwest from 1850-1888. The ruins can be visited on the Hyatt Family Ranch. It is recommended that you visit the Chamber of Commerce in Deming, New Mexico before going out to fort, as they have interesting information. Take State Highway 26 east out of Deming and turn left on exit A019, go past ranch house (out of courtesy, you might let them know you're there, but the gates are apparently always opened), after first cattle guard take an immediate <u>left</u>, and follow around about 2 miles. A pick-up or jeep, or vehicle of such nature is recommended. (Not your wife's new Lincoln!) Look for old cemetery at first welcome sign.

Apache Springs – located in Apache Pass, the Butterfield Trail followed through these rocky and rugged hills. The spring was a major water source and also the scene of many battles between Indians and the cavalry. The spring is located on the hike up to the old Fort Bowie ruins.

Fort Bowie – located off I-10 in eastern Arizona. A distance away you can spot the mountain formation that looks like two heads peeking over the hills, thus the name of the range *Dos Cabezas Mountains*. A nice hike to the site of the ruins takes you past several site markers, the old cemetery (which contains the grave of one of the Apache Chief Geronimo's son, along with several other interesting markers), and the spring. Give yourself time to enjoy the scenery. A minimum of two hours is recommended for a round trip hike, so one might consider a pack lunch, or at least taking some water with you. For those with disabilities, call (520) 847-2500.

San Pedro River – today we hardly notice driving over rivers on our wonderful modern highways with bridges, but in 1865, river crossings were a lot more difficult. One place to cross over the San Pedro is at Benson, Arizona on I-10.

San Xavier Mission – a beautiful old mission that is now a school is located just south of Tucson, Arizona on I-19. There is a gift shop located there and you can visit the chapel.

Tucson – A beautiful southwestern city that was established in 1776 as a military outpost for the territory called New Spain. Several old journals and diaries document the use of the road through Tucson.

The old fort has been partially restored. It later was named Fort Lowell (1866).

Sacaton – now on the Pima Reservation, the site was also mentioned several times in documents as a regular water stop through the southwest.

Maricopa Wells – located south of Phoenix, is now called Maricopa. Military documents mention the Indians there as being on "good terms" with the soldiers, and selling produce to travelers. From this location, travelers of the 19th Century faced 45 miles without fresh water to Gila Bend, the next water stop.

Antelope Peak – Described as a "towering peak some four or five hundred feet tall". Some early documents mention Mexican families living there, while others tell of an adobe building with an attached corral that was used for the stage station. Interstate 8 now is north of the famous peak, but a good view of it and the Table Top Mountains are still picturesque.

Gila Bend (Oatman Flat) – Remembering that travelers followed water routes and rivers, the highway today does not follow the exact route of yesteryear. Gila Bend is on I-8, and is an interesting desert town. Be sure to take time to look around.

Site of Oatman Family Massacre – After leaving Gila Bend, take exit 106 to Painted Rock Park. The host at the Park helped us find the monument about the site. It is about 10 miles on past the entrance. You will actually feel as though you are trespassing as the road goes through the Hanson (Oatman) Farm. It is well worth the trip.

Fort Yuma – Begun as adobe buildings in 1852 on the western bank of the Colorado River, the monument of old Fort Yuma is now on the California side. The city of Yuma today is located on I-8 on the extreme western side of Arizona. Yuma Crossing State Historic Park is the site of the Yuma Quartermaster Depot that was used by the U.S. Army from 1864 – 1883. There is an interesting museum that is a must-see and they can also direct you to the old Fort Yuma monument. Be sure to plan a visit to the Territorial Prison, even though it was built and used later than this story.

Bibliography

American Slave, Supplement Series 1, Vol 1: 13-16. Interviewers Ila B. Prine, Federal Writers' Project, Dist. 2, April 16, 1937, W.P. Jordan, Ruth Thompson, and Travis Jordan, North Carolina District #3.

Beck, Warren A. and Ynez D. Haase, Historical Atlas of New Mexico, University of Oklahoma Press, 1969.

Bushnell, William Addison, Diary of a Civil War Soldier. This diary was copied from a typed and handwritten copy of the original diary by Peter Steelquist, 28 Dec. 1999. This diary was downloaded from the Internet 26 Aug. 2002.

Couchman, Donald H., Cooke's Peak – "Pasaron Por Aqui" (They Passed by Here), Cultural Resources N0. 7, 1990.

Frazer, Robert W., Forts of the West, Norman, OK, University of OK Press, 1965.

Haenn, William, Images of America, Fort Clark and Brackettville, Arcadia, 2002.

Hartley, G.W. "Doc", "Bloody Cooke's Canyon", Desert Winds magazine/Spring 2000.

History of San Elizario and Surrounding Area, typed pamphlet handed out at Mission San Elizario.

The Handbook of Texas, a joint project of The General Libraries at the University of Texas at Austin and the Texas State Historical Assoc.

University of Arizona Library Online, Books of the Southwest.

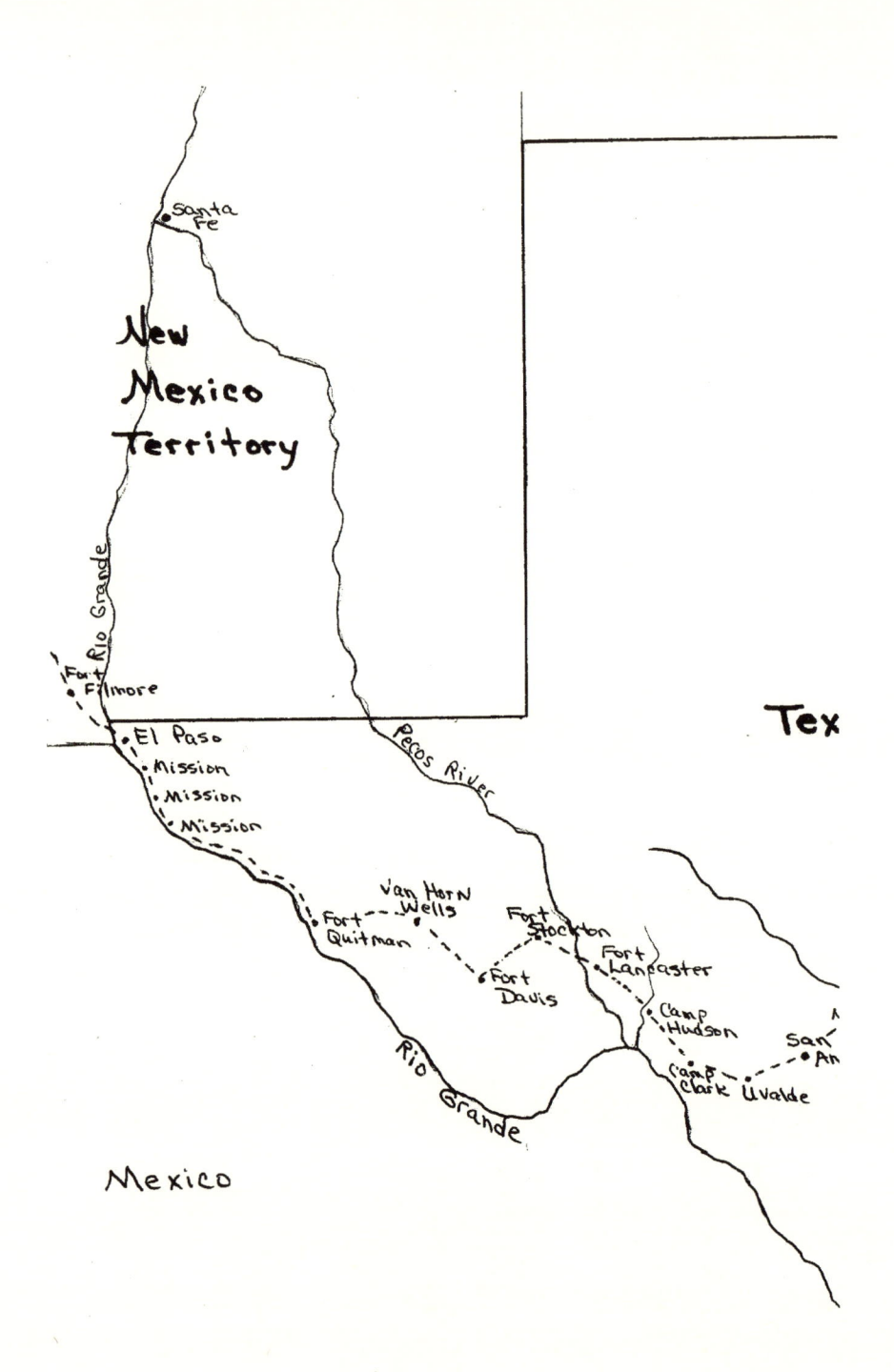

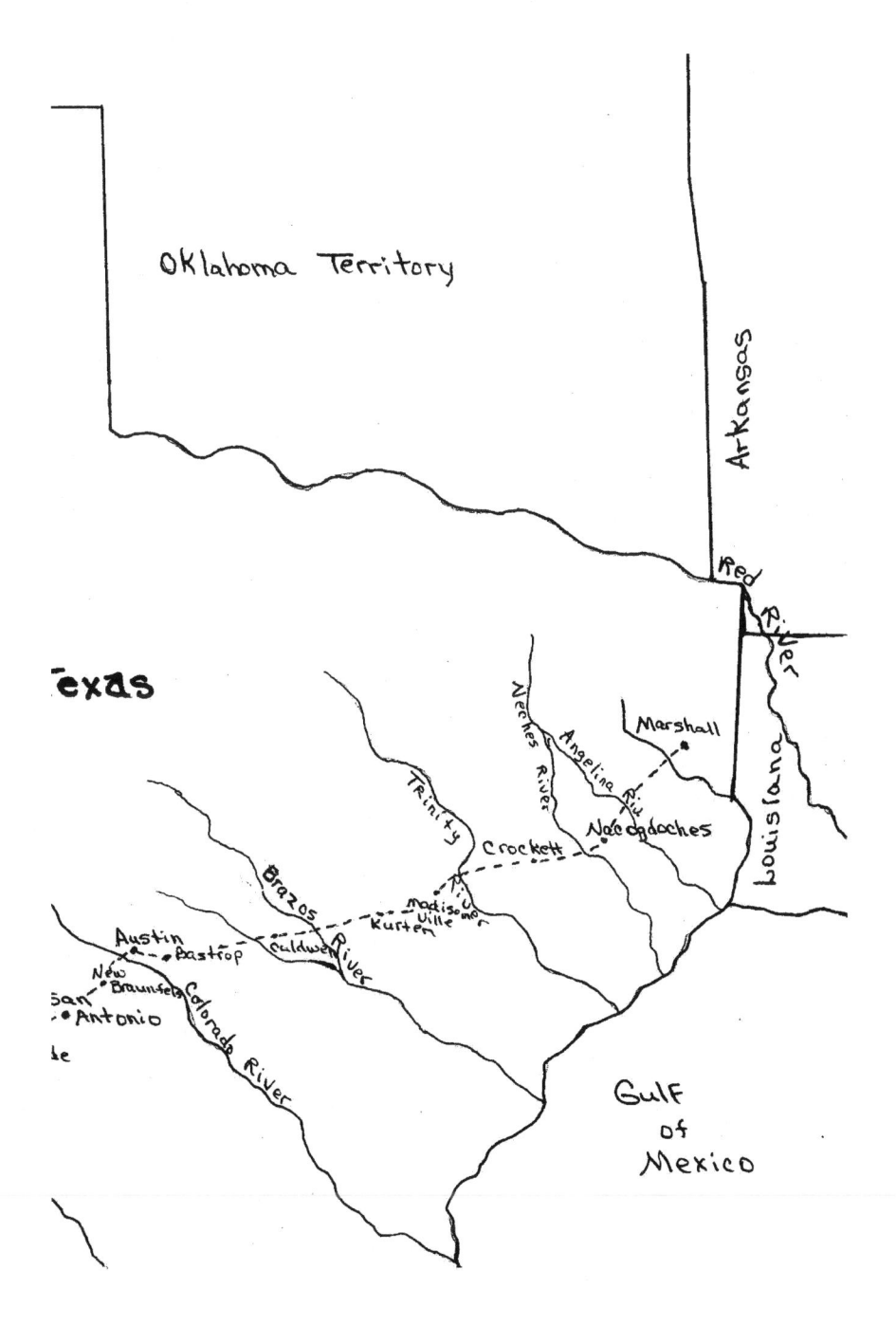

This book is an historical novel, which means the settings are real and the characters fictional. Much research was done so that, anyone that is willing, can follow the road that thousands of earlier people actually traveled. The period of time is at the end of the Civil War, April 1865. Texas was dirt poor, as was most of the South.

An ex-slave and his wife find themselves guardians of a young girl, and on the trip of their lives. Two confederate soldiers and an old army scout end up helping this couple try to deliver their ward safely over almost 1,500 miles of the country's most uninhabitable terrain. They battle tornados, Indian attacks, Comancheros, and many other unimaginable perils. In these times and places, it could have happened just this way.

Come and take the trip with them, and then take your own pilgrimage with the "How to Get There" chapter that is found at the end of the book.

ABOUT THE AUTHOR

Shelia Y. (Davis) Nicholson was born in Illinois, but spent her childhood in Odessa, Texas. She attended Odessa Junior College and Lubbock Christian College, where she met her husband. They now reside in Gallup, New Mexico, where their two children were born and raised.

While her interests are many, her priority's place God first, then comes family and friends and, of course, history. She loves history, especially American history. She spent seven years (as time allowed) researching Civil War and post Civil War people, times, and places for this book.

Made in the USA
Columbia, SC
04 January 2025